THE AWAKENING TETRALOGY BOOK 3

Tranquility

A Village of Hope

A SPIRITUAL BOOK BY

Ken Luball

~ ~

Tranquility: A Village of Hope

"The Awakening Tetralogy" - A Series of Four Spiritual Books, Volume 3

Ken Luball

Published by Ken Luball, 2022.

Registration Number
TX 8-712-350
Effective Date of Registration:
March 04, 2019
Title
Title of Work: Tranquility: A Village of Peace, Love and Hope
Completion/Publication

Year of Completion: 2019
Date of 1st Publication: March 02, 2019
Nation of 1st Publication: United States
International Standard Number: ISBN 9781798429297

Author

• Author: Ken Luball
                                                                  text
Author Created: No
Work made for hire: Citizen of: United States

Copyright Claimant

Author's Note

Nestled deep in the Canadian Rocky Mountains lies Tranquility, a hidden village where peace, wisdom, and spiritual awakening are part of everyday life. In this third installment of 'The Awakening Tetralogy', young Elke is born into a community unlike any other—surrounded by enlightened souls from Tranquility and a neighboring First Nations village.

As she journeys through life, Elke shares the powerful spiritual lessons passed on to her—lessons about love, ego, truth, and inner peace. Through simple storytelling and profound insight, 'Tranquility: A Village of Hope' gently invites readers to reflect, awaken, and reconnect with their true self.

As you prepare to begin your search for meaning, do so with an open heart and mind, ready to delve deeper into the mysteries of existence. Let us embark on this spiritual adventure together, with the third of this four book series of spiritual novels, and, in doing so, discover the answers you are searching for.

Imagine

Imagine there's no heaven,
It's easy if you try,
No hell below us,
Above us only sky,
Imagine all the people,
Living for today.
Imagine there's no countries,
It isn't hard to do,
Nothing to kill or die for,
And no religion too,
Imagine all the people,
Living life in peace.
You may say I'm a dreamer,
But I'm not the only one,
I hope someday you'll join us,
And the world will be as one.
Imagine no possessions,
I wonder if you can,
No need for greed or hunger,
A brotherhood of man,
Imagine all the people,
Sharing all the world.
You may say I'm a dreamer,
But I'm not the only one,
I hope someday you'll join us,
And the world will live as one.
- John Lennon -

Table of Contents

Chapter 1: The Village of Tranquility

Chapter 1:
The Village of Tranquility

M

y name is Elke. The story I am about to tell you is about my remarkable journey through life.

I was born in the spring of 1972 as the first rays of the early morning sunrise began to flicker over the nearby mountaintops. My parents were part of the hippie generation; that will explain much of what I am about to share with you. My story is about a world few know about. It is about a village called Tranquility, which is a place of hope, where all the existing negative problems of the world are rarely witnessed. It is a place where everyone has respect for each other and where love and compassion abound, without any ulterior motives. You may believe no such village could ever exist, but I assure you it does. It is hidden away deep in the mountains, isolated from the complexities living in the wider world brings.

My parents started this community with four of their friends they met at the Woodstock Music Festival in the summer of 1969. In the ensuing years, many others were to join them in their endeavor to create a home where everything is shared, including love. The love I am talking about is not romantic love, but rather spiritual love, freely shared with and among others. It is a place where there is no loneliness and success depends on each of us contributing to help each other succeed.

Tranquility is located deep in the Canadian Rocky Mountains. The only way to reach our village is by using a 4-wheel drive vehicle, driving over an old fire road winding through the mountain passes. Our town is located about 60 miles northwest of Banff in Alberta, Canada. Tranquility is beautiful, surrounded by the high peaks of the Rocky Mountains, which remain snow-clad for most of the year. A stream, beginning near the top of one of the mountain peaks, flows through our village, adding to the idyllic surroundings.

There are even fish in the stream we eat, cooking them up over a fire shortly after we catch them for a delicious meal.

The town of Tranquility was founded almost 50 years ago, at the height of the hippie revolution in the early 1970s. Though it had only six people when it was founded, it has since grown to almost 1000 people, including the children born here and their children as well.

The reason I am writing this story is to let you know it is possible to live a life that is selfless, in which caring and compassion for others take precedence over worry about one's own survival. Until I was 21 years old, this was the only place I had ever lived. I had experienced a little of what the world was really like on our excursions into Banff, where we would buy some of our supplies and sell some of the crafts we had made, and surplus produce we had grown in the garden.

When I turned 21, I developed a strong desire to see what the world was really like, beyond the isolated shelter of our community. So, shortly after I turned 21, I traveled to New York City, where I was to stay with my uncle for almost a year. After that year, before returning to Tranquility, I decided to take a walkabout; for the next year, I traveled, with my best friend, to different parts of the world. I will discuss those trips later in my story.

It was hard for me to truly understand how difficult life must be for everyone else who did not live in Tranquility. From the many stories my parents and others in the village had told me about life elsewhere, it appeared to me the world was a very harsh dangerous place to live in. When we were in Banff, I would often visit the library, where I could read about what was going on in the world. I read about wars, homelessness, fear, hunger, global warming, prejudice, and so much more. It was heartbreaking to know so many were struggling just to survive each day. They often seemed to be on their own, not having anyone, but a few family members, to help them when challenges arose in their life.

Life is so different in Tranquility. Though now there are almost 1000 inhabitants, everything is shared. No one is alone, for in our community, we help each other. The story I am going to tell you is about my life and what life could be like for everyone if only we sincerely cared and helped each other, rather than competing to survive in the world. Life does not have to be so difficult. The many struggles others have faced, and I read about in the library in Banff, do not have to happen if we only replace fear with love and selfishness

with selflessness. This is a part of the DNA of each resident living in the small communal village of Tranquility, where I have lived my entire life.

My parents and their friends believed it was possible to express universal love and live a meaningful life in which everything is shared equally. With their friends, they traveled around North America, looking for an ideal spot to start a community far away from all the problems and distractions of the world. The war in Vietnam was ongoing at this time in history, as were the civil rights struggles, a result of discrimination against those who were not white and did not look like the people who ran the country. These and many of the other struggles my parents witnessed in the world made them decide to leave this world behind.

This story about Tranquility is the story of a village of hope, almost 50 years after its creation. It is a story of living in a world of love, caring, compassion, respect, sharing, and togetherness and one I hope will show you what is possible if only we are able to change our fundamental beliefs about the world and how we treat each other.

I Have a Dream

I have a dream of a world where love is selflessly shared with all others. It is a world where there is no hunger, homelessness, or endless war; no greed, prejudice, or inequity. A world where few of the many problems and harmful emotions defining humanity's existence are present.

Our world is at a precipice. To achieve such a dream, and make it a reality, we must each decide to embrace love over fear. You may not believe such a dream can come true, but I assure you it can. All we lack is the will, belief, and sincere desire to make this dream real.

Chapter 2:
Growing Up in Tranquility

I was born at home on a quiet spring day in the log cabin my parents had built earlier that year. I was the oldest of three children and, from what I now understand, I was brought up very differently from most children elsewhere in the world. Besides my younger brother and sister, a raccoon and wolf cub lived with us as well.

I have always loved animals. From what I can recollect of my first memories, I was not afraid of any animal, not even those I should have been afraid of like bears and mountain lions. Instead, whenever I saw an animal, I ran up to it, waving my arms and laughing. That is how we ended up with our two pets. They wandered into our village when they were very young, both barely a month old. My parents told me their mothers were probably killed and they most likely would not live since they were so small and had no one to look after them. Though I was only two years old, I begged my parents to let me keep them since I did not want them to die. I told them I would feed them, and they could sleep with me every night. My parents also loved animals like I did, and so they said the two could live with us, but it was my responsibility to take care of them.

The raccoon cub came to us first; he was cold, hungry, and afraid. We named him Rocky, after the Beatles' song Rocky Raccoon, which my parents really liked. When he first showed up, I fed him as soon as we got home and held him in my arms almost the entire day. When I went to sleep, I even put him in my bed; he was so cozy to cuddle with. We became best friends, often playing together all day.

We found the wolf cub about a month later. Her leg was injured when she wandered into our village, all alone, shivering, and afraid. My parents brought her back to our cabin, where they tended to her wound. Rocky was very interested in our new visitor; they both appeared to get along very well. I did not even have to ask my parents if I could keep her, since my mom immediately fell in love with her. Our First Nations neighbors happened to be visiting our village that day. We asked them what the word for wolf was in the Cree language, to which they replied, Mahihkan. So that is how our tiny wolf cub got her name.

Both of these animals were now our pets, and they lived with us throughout their lives. They both slept with me in my bed – Rocky slept by my feet and Mahihkan by my head. I think Mahihkan thought she was my mother, as she frequently licked and nuzzled me.

Though I lived in my parents' house, everyone in Tranquility helped bring me up; in our village, all the children were brought up by the community. Everyone shared responsibility when it came to teaching us about life. Not only did they tell us what was good about life, they also told us if we did something wrong. It was like we had many sets of parents; each adult was involved in all the children's education and upbringing. We learned so many things, but the primary underlying lesson delivered to us was always about respecting each other and all life. This included not only people but also the many animals and plants sharing the forest mountains with us. We were taught every life is special, regardless of whether that life was a person, animal, or plant. We were also taught to respect Mother Earth, as we share a symbiotic relationship with her; the earth relies on us as much as we rely on it.

We had a very large garden, where we grew all our vegetables during the short growing season in the Canadian Rockies. Everyone worked in the garden, as we had to grow enough food during the few warm months to last all year. We also planted many fruit trees that grew well at higher altitudes; we had peaches, cherries, apricots, pears, apples, as well as other fruits. Our fruit harvest was not always very good though, as the buds and flowers would often get damaged during an early spring frost. When we knew a spring frost was coming, everyone in the village would cover the trees and light fires, which were set in smudge pots filled with oil, and kept going through the night near the trees to keep the buds from freezing and dying.

It was the job of all the children to not only help plant everything in the spring but also to harvest the vegetables and fruit when they were ready. I loved doing this; it was gratifying to watch everything grow throughout the summer, knowing we would have enough food for everyone to eat throughout the year. We also fished in the stream flowing through our village and in the nearby river the stream flowed into. We ate a lot of fish, mostly trout, some whitefish, and, at certain times of the year, salmon, when they swam upstream in the nearby river. Our diet mostly consisted of fish, vegetables, and fruit, which was not only very healthy but also thoroughly sustained us.

As for living arrangements, together everyone built separate houses. For the older children, who were ready to live on their own, there was a dormitory-like building where they would live and sleep under one roof. By the time someone was old enough to be living away from the house they grew up in, they were quite self-sufficient. Since we were all brought up knowing how to do everything, it seemed natural to move out at this age. Most of us, as I did, moved into the communal dormitory on our 16th birthday. This was a signal we were adults and could survive in the world by ourselves.

Tranquility also had a building where we attended school; it was here we learned to read, write, and all the other skills we would need to survive in the world, should we decide to leave the village when we were old enough.

Besides learning all the things we needed to know to survive in the mountains, the primary lesson we learned was how to treat others and respect all life. We also learned the importance of sharing, compassion, giving, selflessness, love, empathy, and so much more. We were brought up to understand no one was better than another, regardless of who they were or what they looked like. If, for any reason, we did not treat others this way as we were growing up, we were gently reminded why it was important to do so. We were taught to treat others like we wanted to be treated ourselves.

This was not only true of each other, but for all life as well. Nothing was taken for granted. Survival in this harsh environment meant we all had to work hard every day if we were to stay warm in the winter and have enough food to eat all year round. From the moment we were born, we were taught about the importance of the community and everyone in it. We were also taught to share everything equally. Success, we were told, can only happen when everyone succeeds together; it can never happen if only you succeed yourself.

Being brought up this way, I was able to experience love; not the artificial love you may have read about or seen in the movies, but true love. This is a love that comes from the heart, where our spirit exists. True love is given freely without expectation of getting anything in return. If you were lucky enough to be brought up as I was, then your life will be full of love, happiness, and meaning.

We are Each Other's Teachers

Every person we meet, regardless how brief, affects our life. A small part of their spirit, their essence, remains with us, changing, if only slightly, the direction our life will take. Each one of us, therefore, may change the world by sharing our authentic self, our spirit, with others.

We are each other's teachers. Let us, therefore, make certain the unconditional loving messages we share always help others, rather than harm them, leaving our children a world of hope, rather than despair.

Chapter 3:
In the Beginning

I always loved to hear the stories my parents and their friends told us about their first year when they arrived at the Canadian Rockies. It sounded like life was very hard for them as they learned how to survive away from civilization. What I am about to tell you are fragments from the many stories we all grew up hearing, about life when the village of Tranquility first began.

In the late 1960s, there was discontent throughout the United States. My parents first met at an anti-war demonstration in Washington, D.C., in 1968. It was there, in support of both the civil rights movement and in defiance of the Vietnam War, they and thousands of others came together to try to change the direction our country was going in. They all had long hair, liked classic rock and roll music, smoked marijuana throughout the day, and believed in the hippie values and beliefs many younger people had at that time. The protestors were peaceful, though they were often met with tear gas and billy clubs; those in power at the time, like at any other time, did not want anyone disagreeing with them. My parents were arrested, beaten, and gassed for their efforts, but they, as did so many of their generation, believed so strongly change was needed. they continued to protest the unjust society in which they lived.

It was not all bad though; my parents also went to Woodstock in 1969, an event which changed their lives forever. It was after that music festival, with two other couples they met at the concert, they decided to leave and begin their lives anew in the Rocky Mountains in Canada. I was to find out later the reason they ended up in Canada was because the government drafted my father to go to Vietnam; he was a conscientious objector though, and refused to go. Rather than go to jail for dodging the draft, they decided, instead, to move to Canada. With their four new friends they had met at Woodstock, they drove around, living in an old Volkswagen Bus, as they searched for a new beginning in Canada. In the early 1970s, they visited the beautiful city of Banff, in Alberta, surrounded by the majestic snow-capped Rocky Mountains. It was then they decided they would settle in this area. Driving northwest from Banff, they eventually found a rugged fire road, which they followed for many miles. Near a clearing in the woods with a stream flowing through it, they decided, with their four friends, it was here they would begin their new life. In the isolation and beauty of these mountains, they would put down roots and live with nature.

By the time they arrived at what was to become the village of Tranquility, it was early spring of 1971 and there was much to be done to prepare for the harsh winter awaiting them in just five or six months. They knew they were going to have to build homes for themselves, so they brought tools to build log cabins. They also brought seeds to plant a garden, so they would have food to eat when the seasons changed.

The first six settlers of Tranquility grew up in cities and knew very little about how to survive in the isolated wilderness of the Canadian Rocky Mountains. Luckily, my grandfather, who I never met, was a carpenter and all-around handyman; when my father was growing up, he taught him how to build almost anything. My mother also used to spend her summers at her grandparents' farm in upstate New York, where she learned how to plant and harvest different crops. Though they struggled that first year, they were able to plant a large garden in the spring with the many seeds they brought with them; they, of course, also planted a marijuana crop as well.

The first year was very busy as the garden had to be cleared and hand tilled before they were able to plant their seeds. They also had to cut down many trees to build a log cabin big enough for all six of them to live in through the first winter. They knew they would not have time that year to build three homes, so all their efforts were put into building one large cabin that would withstand the freezing weather and protect all of them from the cold, snow, and unknown dangers living in the wild brought. The cabin was meticulously built, as my father notched out the end of the logs, so they snugly fit together. The original cabin they built still exists today; it is currently being used as the schoolhouse where the children go every day to learn. Between the garden, building the log cabin, storing wood to burn in the winter, and building a root cellar for the vegetables they were growing, they all kept very busy from early in the morning until sunset.

They also ate a lot of fish. The stream, flowing through Tranquility, was full of fish, especially trout. My father devised an ingenious trap he placed across the stream, which would trap the fish as they swam by. They were therefore able to catch and eat so many fish, they never lacked food. Since all the original settlers of Tranquility did not eat meat, believing animals have a spirit within them as well, their diet during those early years, and even today, consisted primarily of fish and vegetables. They also brought seeds to plant trees for fruit, which, after about ten years, began yielding enough produce to harvest.

It was hard work, yet they told me it was joyful. They loved being in the mountains where no one else lived. They also loved watching all the animals they saw as they were busy each day. Every day, they cut down many trees and stripped them of their bark, so they could be used to build the cabin they would live in. While the men were building the cabin, the women worked hard as well, cultivating, and planting a large garden in the clearing by the stream. Everyone helped each other; there was a lot needing to be done. But this did not mean there was no time for a bit of fun. They would often swim in the nearby river, play guitar, and sing by a fire under the bright, star-lit night sky. The sounds of the trees blowing, water rushing by in the stream, animals in the forest, and sight of the crystal-clear sky, filled with stars as far as the eye could see, mesmerized them as they watched the flames from a fire they had built jump high into the night sky. A more perfect life could not be imagined.

During many of those beautiful starry nights, they often talked until dawn about their spiritual beliefs. Over those summer nights, during the first year in Tranquility, they came to understand a lot about spirituality and unconditional love. As I was growing up, not a single day went by when these beliefs were not discussed. They shared their spirituality not only with all their children, but with everyone who visited our village throughout the years as well. What I am about to tell you, about my understanding of spirituality, is what has been passed down to me over the years by my parents, everyone in our village, and from our First Nations neighbors, the Cree.

A spirit resides within everything alive. The spirit has had many names over the years, though it represents an ethereal entity meant to guide us through our life. In our village, the spirit is not differentiated from god or the soul; all three are considered equal and synonymous. This guide is eternal, present before, during, and after our lives have ended. All the answers we seek about life are within us, where the spirit exists. To know and understand how our lives should be led, simply sit quietly, close your eyes, quiet your mind, and listen. Though this may sound easy to do, I assure you it is not. From my earliest memories, meditation was a large part of both my life and everyone else's who lived in Tranquility.

The message of the spirit has to do with unconditional love, which is love given without expectation of receiving anything in return. Only positive qualities are associated with the spirit, including compassion, empathy, happiness, love, and selflessness. To find true happiness and meaning in your life, all you must do is listen quietly and follow the advice of your spirit.

This is often very difficult to do though. For within us is also another guide, created when we are first born, and which remains with us until the day we die. My parents called this guide the self. The self or ego represents everything we learn in life, including everything we are taught that allows us to survive in the world. Though the self is important to help us fit in and follow society's rules, it is also the cause of most of the emotional and psychological problems, as well as many physical illnesses we encounter throughout our lives. Negative emotions such as hate, fear, anger, jealousy, prejudice, and selfishness are often associated with the self. We were taught stress, anxiety, and depression often result from the conflict between the spirit and self. This tug of war goes on within us every day and is the cause of many of the problems experienced by many each day.

Outside our idyllic village, people are taught success and happiness can be found outside themselves, in the world. They learn money, prestige, and material things will bring happiness and meaning in their lives. However, nothing could be further from the truth. True happiness can never be found in the world, where the self tells us it is found. It may only be found within each of us, where the spirit is present. Though the self is important in helping us survive and navigate in the world, understanding, happiness, love, success, and meaning may never be found there.

My parents described two paths in life we may pursue: the path of the spirit or that of the self. The path of the spirit leads to genuinely finding meaning and happiness in our lives. This is the path in life we are meant to follow.

The other path, that of the self, is the cause of war, misery, fear, hate, starvation, homelessness, climate change, prejudice, depression, anxiety, selfishness and so much more. This was a path the original settlers of

Tranquility decided they could no longer follow. They therefore decided that first summer, they would only follow the true path of the spirit.

Though the cabin was finished before the cold first set in and their first harvest was quite successful, nothing could have really prepared my parents and their friends for that first winter. It was extremely harsh with tons of snow. They had cut and split a lot of wood to cook with and burn for heat, though, as it turned out, it was not enough to keep them warm throughout the season. Since they all grew up in cities, they were simply not prepared for what was to come. Their clothes were not warm enough and they had to ration their food, since they were afraid they may not have enough to last until spring. They kept busy during the short winter days, reading, playing music, and talking about spirituality. It was during that first winter I was conceived, or so I have been told; after all, my parents told me, they had to stay warm somehow. In January, they began to run out of wood for the fire as well as food to eat. My father and the others, therefore, had to go out in the cold to cut and split wood each day.

That month, my parents first met our neighbors, who lived about ten miles northwest of us. These neighbors were an indigenous Cree tribe of the First Nations, who had lived in their village for several generations. One day, as they were hunting moose[1], caribou[2], rabbit[3], and other animals that lived among us in the mountains, they luckily stumbled upon our cabin. It was a miracle, for at the time they came, everyone was growing very anxious, wondering if they would be able to survive through the winter. Fortunately, there were two children in the hunting party who could speak a little English, so they were able to understand each other. My parents and their friends explained to them why they were living there, their hope to begin a new life and their concern about surviving through the winter. The hunting party from the First Nations village, who found our cabin, took pity on them, and invited my parents and their friends to return with them to their village. There, they could get food and warm clothes, which they made from the hides of animals they had hunted. The original settlers happily accepted their invitation.

While at the Cree village, my mother was four months pregnant with me. My parents stayed in the teepee of the village Shaman, while the other two

---

1.   https://www.thecanadianencyclopedia.ca/en/article/moose/

2.   https://www.thecanadianencyclopedia.ca/en/article/caribou/

3.   https://www.thecanadianencyclopedia.ca/en/article/rabbit/

couples stayed with two other families. The Shaman or medicine man was a holy person who possessed tremendous power and knowledge. He healed the sick, interpreted dreams and visions, and led ceremonies. He also prayed to the Great Spirit, decided when to hunt, tried to change the weather, and even predicted the future. When called upon to help someone who was ill, he smoked tobacco, sang songs, danced, burnt sage and sweet grass, and prayed to the spirits. They also met a medicine woman in the tribe who knew which herbs and plants to use for healing. These plants were collected and stored in containers and were used to successfully treat many illnesses and injuries.

That winter, while at the First Nations village, the original settlers of Tranquility became great friends with many members of the tribe. They began to learn each other's language and spent many hours talking about their spiritual beliefs. The two children they first met, who spoke a little English, were quite helpful in these discussions, though by the time my parents and their friends returned to Tranquility that spring, the two groups could communicate well enough to at least be understood.

Art and music constitute important elements of Cree culture. During those three months at the First Nations village, my parents and their friends learned how to cook traditional native Cree dishes as well as make beautiful clothes, pottery, and crafts, which they would later sell in Banff during the summer tourist season. They would then be able to use the money they made from selling their crafts to buy tools, seeds, oil for a generator, and other items needed in the village.

The Cree believe everything in the world is alive, possesses a soul, and exists in harmony with each other. They also believe the spirit is eternal and when we die, only our physical body dies. After death, our journey, the spirit's journey, continues. They understand people and nature are connected, and happiness is only achieved by living a life in balance with nature.

Most of their traditions, songs, and prayers were shared orally by the Elders. The Elders were wise and respected and were the storytellers, teachers, and spiritual guides of the tribe. My parents and their friends learned much about Cree culture from the Elders during that first winter, and it had a profound influence on their overall spiritual beliefs.

They also observed many of the Cree rituals and ceremonies. Over the years, when we would visit our First Nations neighbors, we would observe the

Sun Dance[4], powwows[5], feasts, pipe ceremonies, sweat lodges[6], and much more. Often, drums and flute music accompanied the dancing, and when I was older, I would also accompany them with my guitar, which my parents taught me to play at a very young age.

The Cree also believed in the Great Spirit or Creator. The Great Spirit exerted power over all things –animals, plants, humans, and even stones and clouds. The sun, which gave the earth light and warmth, possessed great power as well. The earth was considered the mother of all spirits. Mother Earth provided everything they needed to survive. They took only what they needed and lived in balance and harmony with all of creation. They harbored a deep respect for the land, the plants, and the animals. They believed they were put on this land to protect and look after it. Animals played an important part in their lives. When they hunted game for food, a prayer was offered to the spirit of the slain animal.

The six friends remained in the First Nations village for almost three months, until the gentle whispers of spring started to reveal themselves. Then, the six original settlers of Tranquility left the Cree village, anxious and a little afraid, and returned to their log cabin.

My parents had become great friends with the Shaman's family during that winter. So much so that after I was born, their teepee became my second home. The Shaman's wife was also pregnant during that first winter and gave birth shortly after I was born to a daughter, who they named Hurit, which means beautiful in the Cree language. They also had a one-year-old son named Noodin, which meant wind. As their parents later explained to me, Noodin was born on a very windy day in the middle of fall.

Hurit and Noodin were to become my best friends as I was growing up. I was always welcome to stay at their home, just as both Hurit and Noodin were always welcomed at my home in Tranquility. We had many adventures and a lot of fun together; I will talk about some of these adventures in a little while.

During the first few years they lived in Tranquility, the original settlers learned to appreciate many of the traditions of the First Nations village. They eagerly danced to drum music and loved to smoke the peace pipe, which was

4.   https://www.thecanadianencyclopedia.ca/en/article/sun-dance/

5.   https://www.thecanadianencyclopedia.ca/en/article/powwow/

6.   https://www.thecanadianencyclopedia.ca/en/article/sweat-lodge/

filled with a harsh tobacco. They did bring along several ounces of marijuana when they went to the village and, occasionally, would substitute marijuana for the tobacco when the pipe was being passed around. I was told the First Nations villagers appeared to really like the tobacco my parents smoked and would laugh endlessly throughout the night on those special occasions.

My parents also brought along a guitar, which they would play for hours while they were there. Both my parents played the guitar and sang; they took turns throughout the day entertaining their hosts with real music. The music they played was classic rock and roll as well as folk music from the 60s and early 70s. I do not think the First Nations villagers had ever heard such music before, though they were very kind and listened quietly, with a smile on their faces. From the moment I could pick up a guitar, I too learned to play and sing those classic songs as well.

Thankfully, due to the kindness of the First Nations tribe, my parents and their friends were able to survive that harsh first winter and learn how to survive on their own in the isolated wilderness of the Canadian Rocky Mountains for many winters to come.

We are All Connected

We live in a self-centered world, worrying only about ourselves and our own success. Accepting this path through life, we are alone, surrounded by a sea of people, separated from each other, passively accepting the disparities living in such a world brings.

It need not be this way. We are all connected. By embracing our common bond, the spirit, a piece of god present within each life, and selflessly helping others in need, everyone may thrive, allowing each to discover meaning in their life as well.

Chapter 4:
Life in Tranquility

I should tell you about our log cabin and all the buildings in Tranquility. We did not have electricity, so we lived as many of the pioneers did a hundred years ago. We heated our cabin with wood, which we harvested from the forest around us every spring and summer. We would then split the wood into smaller pieces and stack it so it would season and dry over the warmer summer months.

As you can imagine, the fall and cooler weather came quite early every year. We cooked using a wood burning stove, and for extra light, we had lanterns, which used oil we would buy when we traded our crafts and extra food we grew, in Banff. We even had an outhouse which we had to use even during the cold winter months. Life was so simple in Tranquility and, to be honest, none of the children who lived and were born there knew any different.

I was born at home in my parents' log cabin on a gentle, cool, spring morning in 1972. By the time I was born, my parents had been living in Tranquility for almost a year. Over the next 21 years, our town grew to include many other children born there as well. It also included many others who heard about our town and moved here to escape the problems of the world beyond the mountains. People of all colors, religions, and beliefs lived among us, but none of that mattered. Tranquility was a commune; it was an idyllic community where everyone respected and cared about each other. There was no competition or judgments here; there was only unconditional love, and everyone was welcome.

It was interesting growing up in a community such as ours and with others who had similar beliefs. As I was to find out, the harmonious views found in Tranquility about the world, Mother Earth, and how all life should be treated were quite different from the beliefs of others who lived outside our spiritual community.

We were brought up understanding the importance of spirituality, which is quite different from traditional religious beliefs. Our community had a strong belief in god, though we did not practice or believe in any organized religions found in the world today. We embraced the belief that god exists within all living things, including people, animals, and plants, and is present in the universe itself. We were brought up to believe a small piece of god exists within each of us and represents the good that resides within. It was our goal in life, the meaning of our life, to become one with god within and share the beauty and love we receive with everyone and with all life selflessly. If I had to define god, I would say god is the totality of all life combined. We do not differentiate between god, soul, or spirit; instead, we accept all three as one and the same.

I, as were all the children in Tranquility, was brought up to be very spiritual. I believed in god, though not in the traditional sense. While our Cree neighbors viewed Wakan Tanka or the Great Spirit as the supreme being and their philosophy about spirituality and god was a bit different from ours, we did share some similar beliefs.

During many of our spiritual conversations in Tranquility, which we had daily with others living there, we also learned the effect our upbringing had on us. We were taught what we learned from observing others and from following the norms of the society we live in affects our views and actions throughout our lifetime. Unfortunately, though our socialization, as my parents called it, is important so we may survive in the world, it is also the cause of much of the confusion, problems, anxiety, illness, and depression so many people experience today and have throughout history. We understood these afflictions and problems were caused by the conflict between our spirit, which comes from within, and socialized self, which is formed by what we learn in the world after we are born. Our goal was thus to lead a life directed by our spirit, learning to ignore the many false paths the socialized self tries to have us follow instead. We are spiritual beings on a human journey. The meaning of life is to accept this truth and allow the spirit within to influence our decisions throughout our lives.

I never truly understood anything except the spiritual path until I left Tranquility. It was only then I saw firsthand the results of what living in an egoistic world are, where the socialized self dominates the thoughts and actions of almost everyone I met. Though I was taught in school and by my parents about this, until I was able to experience it for myself, I simply did not believe or understand why anyone would choose to live this way.

By the time I was five years old, many of the ideas and teachings I had already acquired became a part of who I was to be throughout my life. I was taught in school what we learn before this age becomes the very fabric of the person we will become. At this tender age, I knew nothing about the learned path those who live outside Tranquility follow; I only knew the path of the spirit, of unconditional love.

I also learned the importance of respecting each other, nature, and the animals we shared the mountains with. To stay alive, I understood it was important we all work together selflessly, so we all may be able to survive. I learned to show kindness and understanding to everyone. Everyone and everything was my teacher. I learned not only from my parents but from everyone who lived both in our town and in the Cree village as well. I also learned from the animals and the visitors who passed through our town throughout the years.

We shared the mountains with grizzly and black bears, mountain goats, beavers, moose, caribou, bighorn sheep, elk, deer, wolves, and many smaller animals such as porcupines, chipmunks, ground squirrels, and marmots. There also were others we met in Banff who, like us, simply wanted to escape the madness of modern life, as well as trappers and mountain people. As I was growing up, they would visit us occasionally to escape the loneliness of living in the wild by themselves. Everyone was welcome in our town, and they were all greeted with love and kindness. I was brought up understanding helping each other selflessly was the fundamental basis for not only surviving in the world, but also for finding inner peace and happiness.

I loved when we would get visitors, for they would tell us stories about what life was like outside our town. They often grew up in cities and towns in Canada and the United States and, having become disillusioned with the competitiveness and loneliness of life there, simply left to pursue a simpler life in the mountains. Some of these mountain travelers would join our community, but others preferred the isolation and quiet of living alone. They would pass through our town, not only to visit, but also to trade their furs, in exchange for supplies they would need to survive in the mountains.

We traded with the Cree village as well. I was always excited and loved it when we went to visit them; my parents, by this time, had become good friends with many of the villagers who lived there. Among the many stories we heard as I was growing up was one about how the First Nations tribe helped my parents and their friends the first winter they moved here. My parents told me they most likely would have died that first winter, if not for the kindness of those who lived in this village.

We also knew only by helping each other would all our lives become not only easier, but meaningful as well. Life is meant to be shared with compassion and unconditional love, and we all accepted this as how life should be. Everyone was welcome in Tranquility, for their presence only made us all stronger.

Though our town was isolated, we did receive a fair number of visitors who were simply seeking answers. When I was younger, I never could understand what answers they were looking for. But as I got older, I began to realize, like my parents and the others who lived in Tranquility, those unable to find their answers or happiness in the outside world, came here looking for their answers instead.

I am sure many of you are wondering what it is really like to be brought up in a communal village. Since I did not know any differently, I thought everyone was brought up to believe as I did. It was not until I was 21 years old and left Tranquility for almost two years that I realized what life was really like outside our village.

From the moment we are born in Tranquility, the two primary underlying themes we are taught are humility and respect. We are taught no one is better than another and all life is sacred and precious. Life is not a competition, but rather something to be shared with everyone. Besides the beliefs we were taught in Tranquility, many of the philosophies from our Cree neighbors also crept into ours as well. We learned to respect Mother Earth and everything living on it. We knew the earth as well as everything on it must be treated with care and respect, so it would continue to sustain us. We also knew all life, including the animals and plants, were equally precious.

There were no words for hate or fear in our vocabulary, only love. Since we did not have to compete to survive or prove we were better than others, there was no reason to hate or fear each other. There was no stealing or other crimes either since everything was equally and selflessly shared. If someone wanted something we had, we gladly gave it to them. Everyone in our village lived in peace and harmony. Wealth was not considered to be a position where you had more possessions than another. Rather, in Tranquility, to be wealthy meant having the love, friendship, and respect of others. In Tranquility, wealth was simply a synonym for love.

As for music, little did the children of Tranquility know there was any other music than classic rock and roll or folk music. Shortly after I was born, we had a generator strategically placed in the center of our village. I think the main reason for the generator was simply to play music, which, of course, consisted of the Grateful Dead, Moody Blues, Beatles, Rolling Stones, Jethro Tull, and the other great rock and roll bands and folk singers from the 1960s and early 70s. I must admit we all loved listening and dancing to this music as I was growing up. We never listened to any other musical groups after the 1970s, since my parents told us any music made after that time was simply not worth listening to.

Both my parents played guitar and sang. They told me from the moment I was able to hold a small guitar in my hands, at the age of two, they began teaching me to play the guitar and encouraged me to sing along with them. I, of course, learned to play and sing many of the classic rock and roll and folk songs my parents and the other villagers loved. I still remember playing and singing the Led Zeppelin song Stairway to Heaven to my parents for the first time when I was five years old. They were so proud of me, their eyes glazed with adoration.

I especially loved to play and sing the beautiful folk songs of the time by Peter, Paul and Mary, Simon and Garfunkel, the Momma's and Papa's, Bob Dylan, Joan Baez, Joni Mitchell, Judi Collins, and James Taylor, among many others. I would take every opportunity to entertain anyone who would listen, and I practiced several hours every day. I also enjoyed playing at the many festivals we attended both in Tranquility and in the First Nations village.

Greeting other people with a smile and hug was very common in Tranquility. As we all knew, love is meant to be shared and we freely shared our love with everyone. I am not talking about sexual love, but rather spiritual love, the love that comes from our heart and Spirit. We freely shared this love easily and naturally. Though wearing clothes was optional, and there were those in our village who preferred not to wear anything, most of us wore some clothing to protect us from the elements. We were not embarrassed by nudity; rather it was simply accepted as a natural part of life.

Lying or taking things that weren't yours was simply not tolerated. After all, there was no need to be dishonest. If somebody wanted something someone else had, they simply had to ask; we were not attached to any material things. Everything in the village was shared freely and equally with everyone.

Our village, of course, grew all their own marijuana and would partake in it often during the day. One day, in the early fall, when I was eight years old, several of us who were taking care of the garden where the marijuana was grown decided we were going to surprise our parents by harvesting the entire marijuana crop. By this time, we all knew how to crop back the plants so they would grow thicker and produce better buds to smoke. We felt we were experts since we were helping in the garden since we could first stand.

On this day, we harvested all the marijuana plants and put them in the shed used to dry and cure the plants. We were all so proud of ourselves we could not wait to tell our parents what we had done. To this day, I remember the incredulous proud look our parents had on their faces when we took them to the shed to show them what we had done. Who would have thought eight-year-olds were so smart? Of course, now that I am older, I realize the look on their faces may not have been joy, since we harvested the plants long before the buds had fully matured.

In our village, anyone could gently remind any child if their actions were not appropriate. Tranquility took to heart the saying, it takes a village to raise a child, as everyone was responsible for helping instill these loving values in the young.

As I was to find out when I was 21 and left Tranquility for two years, my idyllic upbringing was far from normal. I simply could not understand why anyone would want to live in a world where hate, fear, depression, anxiety, and loneliness dominated. I was in for quite an awakening the day I left Tranquility. But I will write more about that later.

How to Raise a Happy Child

To raise a happy child, bring them up to believe in the goodness of life, to share unselfishly, foster respect and love for all others, regardless of any differences there may be between us.

Teach our children to find their path and happiness in life, not in the self-centered world, but from their spirit within instead, then to selflessly share their spirit's innate wisdom and unconditional love with all others.

Chapter 5:
Our Neighbors

T

he First Nations village is a part of the Cree nation; they are known as Nehiyawak in the Cree language and have lived in their village for several generations. Before they built their permanent village, the Cree were a nomadic people, following the seasonal migration of animals in order to obtain meat for food and animal hides and bones for making their tools and clothing. They travelled by canoe in summer and by snowshoes and toboggan in the winter, and they lived in tepees, which were cone or dome-shaped lodges covered in animal skins.

Their diet consisted of fish, large and small game, nuts, berries, roots, and plants. They taught us which plants, berries, and roots were safe to eat; the medicine woman also taught my parents which plants were medicinal and could be used to treat various ailments and illnesses.

My parents and the others learned from them how to tan animal hides to make clothing, as well as how to make beautiful items such as pottery and jewelry. Many in our village made these crafts during the long, cold winter months when they would remain indoors. They would then trade or sell these crafts in Banff when spring came, in exchange for seeds and other items needed by the village. In the summers, we would go to Banff during the weekends to participate in the farmers' market, where we sold a lot of our extra produce, both fruit and vegetables. At the market, we would also sell many of our crafts to the tourists flocking through Banff on their way to the Banff National Park.

After the first few winters, many of the villagers in Tranquility became quite good at producing beautiful crafts, thanks to everything the original settlers were taught by the First Nations tribe that first fateful winter. We sold beautiful colorful coats, jewelry, pottery, and miscellaneous items made from the different trees surrounding our village. My father was especially talented in making beautiful log furniture, which we were able to sell for quite a bit of money.

I became friends with many of the children in the Cree village; I always volunteered to accompany my parents when they would visit the village. It was only located about ten miles from Tranquility, and we would visit each other several times a year. We not only traded with each other but also shared meals, got together to play music, and told stories about the past. I learned so much from our visits and loved spending time with all the Cree children. A few of them became my best friends and, even today, as I am retelling the story of my life, this has not changed.

When I visited our neighbors at their village, I would learn so much from the children; we would play and talk for hours about everything. I would tell them what it was like to grow up in Tranquility and they would tell me what it was like in their village. This was interesting to hear because many of their beliefs were beautiful and fascinating.

In addition to learning about their beliefs, I learned how to shoot a bow and arrow, fish, hunt, and craft different items such as baskets and jewelry. They would often laugh at me when I told them what my parents and the other villagers were like in Tranquility. As I was to discover, Tranquility is not an ordinary village.

When they would visit me in Tranquility, my friends would listen to classic rock and roll and folk music. There were peace signs everywhere and we were all brought up to believe in loving everyone equally. There was no such thing as personal space either since everyone hugged each other frequently. The underlying philosophy of peace and love permeated life in Tranquility.

Most people wore their hair long, wore sandals whenever they could, only wore clothes if they wanted, and almost always had a glazed, stoned smile on their faces, even when working and doing chores. There was no hate, fear, or prejudice; only love, happiness, compassion, and caring. This is how I grew up and, to be honest, I did not know life could be any different. I only began to understand it was quite different on my visits to the library in Banff, when I could read about what life was like elsewhere.

My two best friends were Hurit and her brother Noodin. Their father was the Shaman of the village, with whom my parents stayed the first winter when both our mothers were pregnant. The lifelong friendship our parents developed that winter continued with us. Hurit remains my best friend to this day, and I ended up marrying and having three children with her brother, Noodin, but I will talk about that later.

We did so many things together. We would often spend the night at their village and participate in their sacred ceremonies. I would join the other children, dancing to the sacred drum music echoing throughout the village. Hurit and Noodin's mother even made me a gorgeous, colorful dress and moccasins to wear during the ceremonies. Eventually, the village adopted me, making me an honorary member of their tribe; I was always welcomed by everyone when I visited.

I loved their way of life as well as their beliefs and spirituality. I would spend many nights with Hurit and Noodin's family in their teepee when I stayed at the village. Since I had such a keen interest in what their father did as a Shaman, he always spent time teaching me about his beliefs. He told me the Cree creation story of how the universe was formed. It speaks of how the moon, the sun, the stars, and human beings were formed. He talked about the Creator or Great Spirit and how the Great Spirit created the world and everything in it, as well as how this spirit is also found in all living things.

When Noodin was 13 years old, he went on a Vision Quest. In the First Nations village, a Vision Quest happens when a boy approaches puberty; it marks a boy's transition from childhood to adulthood. He would be sent into the woods alone for several days, praying, fasting, and enduring the elements, while he awaited a vision. This vision becomes his guardian spirit and is often an animal. Noodin prepared for his vision quest by listening to his father tell him what to expect. When it was time for Noodin's vision quest, he was sent off into the mountains by himself.

During this time, he neither ate nor drank anything and spent his time in prayer. Throughout Noodin's vision quest, which lasted four days, he told me he had a dream, a vision, in which a wolf, which was a spirit-being, appeared. Shortly after he had his vision, he returned home and talked with his father, the Shaman, about the meaning his vision revealed.

During the many days and nights I spent with Hurit and Noodin, I began to learn the Cree language. In exchange, I taught them how to speak English. When I was at their village, I would only speak the Cree language; and when they were in Tranquility, they only spoke English. After several years, all of us became quite fluent in each other's language.

At the Cree village, I would often dress in traditional First Nations tribal clothes. I loved wearing the colorful native outfits. When Noodin and Hurit came to stay with me at Tranquility though, I always found the most outrageous tie-dyed clothes for them to wear. I would often laugh at them when I saw them dressed in a tie dye shirt, bell bottom pants, with a peace headband and Arlo Guthrie hat.

I am sure it was a culture shock for all of us when we stayed at each other's villages. Though, to be honest, I am sure the shock was greater for Hurit and Noodin than it was for me. I loved everything about the First Nations village and enjoyed participating in all their rituals and ceremonies. It was great fun, especially after I learned how to speak the Cree language. I fit right in and gladly helped with all the chores while I was there.

As for Hurit and Noodin, I am not certain they felt as I did when they would visit me. Living in a communal village is vastly different from anything they had witnessed before. Clothes were optional or minimal, loud rock and roll music was constantly playing in the background, and many people would smoke marijuana throughout the day. Hurit and Noodin helped me with my chores when they stayed with me. They would help in the garden, carrying and stacking wood, and I even taught them how to trim back the marijuana plants to get the best buds to grow.

One evening, we all went for a walk to the nearby river. Noodin brought with him a peace pipe he had made, and I took along several buds we harvested from the garden earlier that day. With the sound of rushing water, the leaves rustling in the wind, and the howls of various animals in the twilight of the early evening, we shared the peace pipe for the next three hours. It was probably the most fun any of us had ever had; we ended up laughing the entire time, though I have no idea what we were laughing at.

Just as the Cree tribe adopted me, Tranquility adopted both Hurit and Noodin. They loved coming to our village and by the time they were eight, they both spoke English quite well. They participated in all the traditions and events we had throughout the year and even attended school with me when they stayed with us. They also loved to talk about their spiritual beliefs with anyone who would listen, though they too adopted many of the spiritual beliefs of our village as I did theirs. The discussions were extremely lively, as each side thought their beliefs were better.

The most fun we had, though, was when we would play music together. Just as my parents taught me how to play the guitar, Hurit and Noodin's father taught them how to play the flute at a very young age. He had hand carved each of his children a flute when they were born and had taught them how to play it; they both still have their flutes to this day. They learned how to play many of the traditional Cree songs and played their flutes alongside the village drummers during their festivals.

When they stayed in Tranquility with me though, they listened to classic rock and roll music so much they began to play their flute along to the music as well. We spent hours sitting under a tree, near the trickling stream in the village, playing our instruments. They played their flutes, as I played my guitar and sang the classic songs I had learned. They became so good at doing this after several years, they were even able to play their flutes to the music of Jethro Tull. It was glorious to listen to and many of the residents in Tranquility often surrounded us, enjoying the music of a time long gone.

When I stayed in their village, Hurit and Noodin's parents would teach me how to sing some of the traditional songs of their culture. Eventually, I was able to learn how to play and sing some of these beautiful Cree songs on the guitar as well. Just as they would practice with me under a tree when they were in Tranquility, we too sat under a tree at the outskirts of their village and played the flute and guitar to their traditional songs. I even learned how to sing the songs, and we often participated in the Cree ceremonies along with the drummers throughout the years.

And, of course, we danced to the music as we played. It was quite a sight to behold: Hurit, Noodin, and I playing the flute and guitar, singing, and dancing around a large fire under the star-laden sky with everyone from the village surrounding us. Along with the sound of the traditional drum music in the background, these celebrations were quite memorable.

Cree (Nehiyawak) Teaching

As Cree people, we believe in balance between the four parts and four directions of the medicine wheel. These four parts for human beings are the spiritual, physical, emotional, and mental aspects of the self. We need to try and balance these four parts that were given to us in order to function as people.

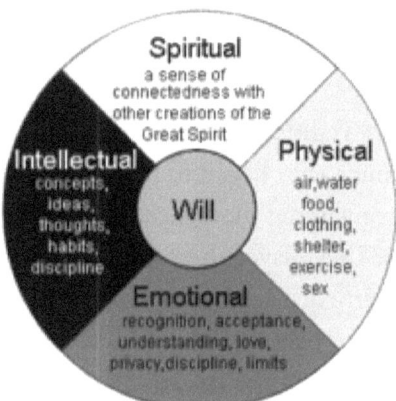

The medicine wheel represents the life journey of people. All life rises and sets like the sun. What we do in between forms our journey. Many people are out of balance because they tend to only favor two realms of self, the mental and the physical. They forget to look after their spiritual side.

Being spiritual is about remembering; it involves remembering that the first thing gifted to you when you came into being was the spirit. Sadly, we tend to forget that, and then neglect our spirit and take it for granted. ~ Elder Mary Lee ~

Chapter 6:
My Upbringing

B
efore I was five years old, all the children played in a small house located near the center of our village. There, several adults spent time with us, not only making sure that we were safe but also teaching us how to treat, be kind to, and thoughtful of each other. We were taught to share everything, the importance of honesty, truthfulness, empathy, and treating Mother Earth and all life on it with the same care we would want for ourselves. There was never consideration for anything else; we all naturally understood this is what life is like. We were reminded the good of everyone was more important than our own selfish desires; we knew we would be able to survive and find happiness and meaning in our lives only if we all selflessly worked together.

I also learned a lot from the Cree villagers. After my parents would visit, I would always stay a few extra days at my best friends' tepee. Since my mother and Hurit's mother were both pregnant with us at the same time, they had a very special bond that was to last the rest of their lives. All our parents thoroughly trusted each other and had no concerns when their children stayed in the other's village. It was like we each had two sets of parents from two very different cultures. For Hurit, Noodin, and I, it was really the best of both worlds. We not only enjoyed being with each other but also enjoyed being a part of each other's culture.

I am sure you are wondering what else we did for fun in Tranquility since we did not have a tv, computers, cellphones, or any of the other electronic distractions children entertain themselves with today. The interesting thing is none of us were ever bored. Besides school, we had plenty of fun things to keep us busy. We played games, not only with each other, but also with many of the children from the nearby First Nations village. We loved to play Pooh Sticks in the stream that ran through our village, seeing whose stick would get to the finish line fastest. We also played tag, hide and seek, baseball, and lots of other games, some of which we learned from the children in the Cree village.

We did chores every day as well, as did everyone who lived in Tranquility. With a few adults supervising, the children were responsible for the garden, which was a very important job. Since we relied on the food we grew to sustain us throughout the year, this was one of the most important jobs in the village. Our garden was huge as the food we grew had to last all year long. We stored much of what we grew in an underground root cellar, located near the garden.

In the early spring, we would help prepare the soil to plant the many seeds we traded for in Banff. After the seeds were planted, we were responsible for weeding and being sure all the plants were well cared for. There was a large fence around our garden to try to keep the many animals out of the garden as well.

Everyone in the village would help harvest the crop in the fall, carefully storing all the vegetables in the root cellar. We also took care of the many fruit trees planted when Tranquility was first settled. By the time I was a teenager, these trees were mostly grown and produced tons of fruit, including peaches, apricots, pears, apples, and other fruits as well. The fruit trees were planted a few miles from our village, in a flat meadow about 1500 feet below Tranquility. Though the original settlers of Tranquility tried to plant the trees closer to the village, they simply would not produce enough fruit; at the lower altitude though, the fruit was plentiful. We shared our fruit with the many animals living in the mountains, though there was plenty left for the rest of us as well.

The children also had to stack the wood the adults began cutting down and splitting in the early spring in order to let it dry. We had to have enough wood to not only heat all the homes in Tranquility through the cold months, but each house also had a wood burning cooking stove. None of us enjoyed this chore, but we all knew it had to be done. Every day, we would all gather where the wood was cut, help the adults bring the split wood back to village, and then stack the wood in rows so it would season and be dry enough to burn when needed. Ironically, in the cool Canadian Rockies, we began burning wood for heat even before fall began and did not stop burning it until just before the following summer.

We also kept busy helping our parents when they were making crafts to sell. We would trade these crafts not only with our neighbors in the First Nations village, but also in Banff at the Farmer's Market, which we visited on the weekends mostly during tourist season in the summer and early fall. There, we sold not only our crafts, but extra fruit and vegetables from the garden as well.

We therefore were never bored when we were growing up; there was always a lot to do keeping us busy.

None of the children really knew what life was like outside Tranquility and the Cree village. As I was to find out many years later, our upbringing was quite sheltered and different from most other children in the world. Others I met during my travels when I was older, were brought up to be fearful and worry only about themselves; the stress, unhappiness, depression, illnesses, anxiety, and loneliness resulting from this type of upbringing was rampant throughout the world. However, by the time I was five, I knew all life, including people, animals, and plants, were important, no one is better than another, and to survive in the world, we need to help each other. I also knew the importance of sharing, humility, responsibility, and to treat all life and Mother Earth with respect.

On the day I turned five, I formally began school. We had a small, one room schoolhouse in a log cabin next to the building where the little kids were. The schoolhouse was the first log cabin built to house the original six settlers of Tranquility. Now that I was five years old, I would join other children to learn how to read and write. We also learned many other things as well; education was very important to our parents.

There were children of all ages here; we had several teachers who would individually teach us our lessons for the day. Not only did the teachers help us learn, but the older children would also help teach the younger ones. We learned not only to read and write, but we also learned about survival, spirituality, love, and much more, though, as always, the underlying theme of community, sharing, and selflessness were communicated to each of us every day.

As we were to learn, however, from some of the visitors to our village, these underlying beliefs were not universal; in fact, they appeared to rarely exist in the world around us. These visitors would tell us about a world where worry, stress, depression, anxiety, hate, and fear existed and where there was only concern for oneself, rather than for each other. It simply did not make sense to us why anyone would choose to live this way.

I had such a wonderful life in Tranquility; we all did. We only knew of honesty, appreciation, thoughtfulness, love, helping each other, and the community. We knew very little of life on the outside, though, from what we heard, it did not sound like a place I would want to live.

Besides the occasional visitors from the outside world, we also had mountain men who lived in the Rocky Mountains year-round visit us as well. This was not an easy life, especially in the winter, but many of them simply had become fed up living in a world where there was so much turmoil. They moved here, looking for the isolation and peace the Rocky Mountains offered, and to enjoy living with the animals and nature. Several of these mountain men became our friends; they would stop by Tranquility to trade and for company. They often did not see anyone else for many months and, especially after the winter, they always looked forward to visiting us.

Everyone was welcome in Tranquility; no one was ever turned away. We gladly shared everything we had with our visitors and looked forward to their visits, almost as much as they did. They told many stories, which we, as children, loved to hear. We believed everything they told us, though, now an adult, I think some of their tall tales were most likely at least partial exaggerated.

My favorite visitor was known only by his nickname, Bear. Bear was a lively character, full of stories from his life before he came to the wilderness, as well as ones of his life living in the Rocky Mountains. Bear had a funny accent, which he told us was Australian. Several years ago, he decided he would take a walkabout. Now, traditionally, a walkabout is a rite of passage among Aboriginal Australians; during this time, teenage males leave their home and live in the wilderness for a period of up to six months to make the spiritual and traditional transition into manhood; this is often a time of reflection.

Though Bear was an adult, he decided he was going to have a walkabout, but instead of remaining in Australia, he decided his walkabout would include traveling around the world. During his travels, he saw parts of Asia, Africa, and South America. But it was when he was in Canada and saw the majestic Rocky Mountains he knew he had found home. He decided as soon as he saw the beauty and isolation these mountains offered, he would remain here and live the rest of his life in nature among the animals.

Bear was almost six feet tall, dark skinned, a bit overweight, and had a full thick beard as well as long hair that went almost halfway down his back. He would bring hides with him from animals he trapped and would trade them for finished clothes we had already made from hides he had traded on his previous visit. He also had a partner in crime that went with him everywhere. Myeengun, which means little wolf in one of Canada's First Nations languages, was a wolf that accompanied Bear everywhere. He had brought him up since he was a cub, orphaned when his mother was killed by a mountain lion many years before.

We all loved when they both visited, but Mahihkan especially loved when Bear would come to visit, since he would always bring along Myeengun. They would play with each other for hours and soon became best friends. Though Bear would only come to Tranquility three or four times a year, they always seemed to remember each other and were excited to see their friend again. All the kids in Tranquility spent many hours playing with Myeengun and Mahihkan and listening to all the tall tales Bear would share throughout his stay.

One of the times Bear visited, Hurit was staying with my family in Tranquility. We both were very curious what life was like in the outside world and attentively would listen to everything Bear said. After Bear left, Hurit and I talked for hours about his adventures, telling each other after hearing about his walkabout, we too would like to see the world. We made a promise to each other one day, we would take a walkabout as well.

We had others who visited us as well; some of them ended up moving to Tranquility permanently. This is partially how our village began to slowly grow. Through word of mouth, others heard about Tranquility at the farmers' market. After they came to visit, they too fell in love with the relaxed atmosphere and decided to move to our village as well. By the time I was 21 years old, there were almost 500 people who lived together, in peace and harmony, in Tranquility.

There was always joy and laughter in our village. Though everyone worked hard, there was always time for humor. We played a lot of practical jokes on each other, constantly trying to outdo one another. Our Cree neighbors also liked to laugh as well, which they often did when they visited us in Tranquility, especially after they smoked our peace pipe. Their Native culture, however, did little to prepare them for what life in a community like ours was like. They would gladly join us smoking our peace pipe, which was filled with marijuana, instead of tobacco. And of course, instead of the beautiful sounds of native drum music, they learned to enjoy the sound of classic rock and roll. Whenever they came to visit, we always made sure our music was turned up as loud as it could go, so they could truly appreciate the sounds of the Grateful Dead and the Rolling Stones.

I also played guitar and sang at many of these events. By now, my repertoire had grown to include quite a few artists and included both classic rock and roll and many folk songs. I would play and sing for hours, entertaining all those who gathered around to hear me. I thoroughly enjoyed performing and loved the feeling of having others enjoy my music. I felt as if I was sharing a part of me with everyone who listened, a part of my spirit, existing within not only me, but everyone else as well. It felt as if our spirits melded together when I sang and played the guitar. I was, therefore, sharing something very intimate with everyone when I was performing.

When I was at the First Nations village, I also learned to dance to the traditional Cree music. I would join the other girls in the village; they taught me how to dance to the sounds of the drumbeat. I always wore the beautiful dress and moccasins Noodin's mother made for me on these special occasions.

In exchange, when they would visit Tranquility, I taught Hurit and Noodin how to dance to rock and roll music. And, of course, I would dress them up in outrageous hippie clothes. We would dance late into the night to the sounds of Led Zeppelin, the Rolling Stones, and Grateful Dead. Occasionally, when the adults were not looking, Noodin would bring his peace pipe and we would fill it with a little marijuana we had taken from our garden when it was being harvested. It was great fun, listening and dancing to music, especially after we had smoked from our peace pipe.

I loved my life. Between Tranquility and my friends in the Cree village, I could not imagine how life could be any better. I not only got my education from what I learned in the classroom, but from everyone who lived in our two villages as well. Everyone was my teacher, and by simply listening and observing, not a day passed which I did not learn something valuable. There was so much knowledge to be absorbed and I readily accepted the collective wisdom others shared.

This extended to the relationships I cultivated as well. Noodin and I had liked each other since we first met when we were small. Though, by the time I was 13 and Noodin was 14, we started to really have feelings for each other. We missed each other when we were not together and thought about each other every day. We loved nature and animals, and we both were extremely spiritual.

Though our spirituality was different, there were many things we agreed on. We would hold hands and take long walks in the surrounding forest, talking for hours about everything under the sun. Noodin would tell me what his beliefs were and what he had learned in the First Nations village. And I, would tell Noodin about what it was like to grow up in Tranquility with parents who lived in a time warp, stuck in the 1960s and 70s. Noodin really liked my parents a lot and always laughed when he would observe the outrageous things he saw when he would visit me.

We were both brought up to respect all life and Mother Earth and to have empathy, be truthful, and have consideration for everyone. Because of this, Noodin and I, though we came from two very different cultures, had much in common. Neither of us knew about hate, prejudice, selfishness, or ever spoke an ill word about someone else. That simply was not tolerated in either of our villages.

As I would find out when I was older, when I visited New York City, and traveled to several different countries around the world, this was not how most children are raised. In fact, outside our two villages in the Canadian Rocky Mountains, I learned Noodin, Hurit, and I and all of those living in our villages were anomalies. Elsewhere, children were raised to be afraid, concerned only for their own survival, rather than others. These qualities, which they were taught from an early age as they grew up, lead to almost all of the problems I observed in my travels throughout the world.

It is possible not to get caught up in this cycle of behavior. I, and everyone in Tranquility, were brought up knowing only positive qualities. Being brought up this way, no one in Tranquility suffered from depression, anxiety, or other illnesses caused from the everyday stress of life suffered from living elsewhere. Also, since Noodin, Hurit, and I did not have any of the many conveniences found in the modern world, such as tv, computers, or cellphones, we simply were never exposed to this part of life when we were children.

Happiness is a reflection of how you are raised. If you are brought up to be only concerned for yourself, accepting the values that instill fear and hate, it may be very challenging to be able to find true happiness or inner peace. If, however, you are brought up knowing only love and do not live your life in fear, the outcome may be very different. We are taught who we are and our basic beliefs in life at a very early age. By then, our beliefs have normally been ingrained within each of us. If, during these early formative years, you learn to accept fear as your primary motivator in life, many of the ills and struggles observed in the world may end up defining you. However, during these early years, if you learn to accept love instead as your guide, many of the pitfalls of living in a modern society may be avoided.

Very little has changed about the philosophy of Tranquility from the time my parents and their friends first came here. Everyone lives and works together selflessly, doing whatever is necessary to assure they all will be able to survive and be happy. There is no loneliness here; everyone in the town is part of a large extended family. There is no competition, hate, prejudice, selfishness, or any of the other negative qualities and emotions often found in the world. Those of us who were born in Tranquility really did not even know what those qualities were, since we had never seen or experienced them, for Tranquility is a 'village of hope'.

We are All Human Beings

Regardless of any comparison dividing us from one another, we are all human beings, each deserving to be treated with respect, empathy, and unconditional love. Though some may think, due to their differences or accomplishments, they are better, their life more important than others, this belief is a lie, perpetrated by the ego, our self-centered beliefs, and is the cause of innumerable hardships experienced by many throughout time.

We are all human beings, equal in every way, regardless of our many distinctions. We are intimately linked together by a spirit, a piece of god, present within each of us. Only by selflessly sharing our spirit's inherent wisdom and unconditional love, without motive or benefit, with all others, will the genuine reason of our life's journey be truly understood.

Chapter 7:
My Life as a Teenager

T

he years seemed to go by very quickly, and before I knew it, I was about to turn 13. By this time, I knew not only how to survive in the rugged Rocky Mountains, but many other things as well. Besides what I learned in school, I also learned how to stay warm, grow food, fish, make clothes, play the guitar, do different crafts, and so much more. Each of us learned how to do everything, since our survival depended on helping each other. We knew we could always rely on each other and would never be alone.

By the time I became a teenager, I understood the importance of Mother Earth and all life blessed to live on it. I also knew to be careful around the many wild animals we shared the mountains with, as well as how to grow and harvest the food we needed to eat throughout the year. We were raised to believe in community and the sacredness of all life, therefore, there was no word in our vocabulary to describe selfishness; it simply did not exist in our community. We instinctively knew, only by working together and helping each other would we be able to survive.

We were also expected to help teach the younger children. Education was very important in Tranquility; every day, each teenager spent time with the younger children, teaching them how to read and write, among many other things. We were now mentors to the little children, as older ones were mentors to us, and as they themselves would be when they were older. It was everyone's job in Tranquility to not only help, but to teach each other to become better human beings as well. By now, all the values of the community were deeply ingrained in me, as they were in all who lived here. I knew I would never be alone in the world, for I had a village to help me and keep me company.

My friends Hurit and Noodin from the Cree village were also central to my world at this point. The three of us always shared a very special bond and thoroughly enjoyed being with each other. They taught me about the Cree culture and history, and I taught them about the communal culture and beliefs of my parents and their generation. I must admit I did not understand why they laughed so much, as I explained to them the culture of peace and love our community believed in.

We had many good times growing up together. We all looked forward to seeing each other throughout the year and would especially enjoy ourselves during the times when celebrations were taking place. We participated in the celebrations of each other's villages throughout the year and would spend many nights staying with each other, getting to not only participate in the celebrations, but also getting to know many of the unique inhabitants of each village.

One tradition we all especially enjoyed was the Harvest Festival. It took place in the fall after the crops from our villages were harvested. Both villages would get together to celebrate the harvest and, each year, we would take turns celebrating the festival in Tranquility or in the Cree village. It was the biggest celebration of the year and it lasted for almost two full days. When the festival was held in the Cree village, we would dance for hours to the traditional drumbeats echoing through the village. We all dressed up in our best clothes and the children wore the traditional clothing of the village we celebrated in. I loved when we celebrated the holiday at the Cree village, since I would get to wear the beautiful dress Noodin and Hurit's mother had made me. Of course, when the celebration was at Tranquility, Noodin, Hurit and all the other children from the First Nations village got to dress up as hippies. It was such fun dressing them up.

And, of course, they got to listen to classic rock and roll music for two whole days. Though I really do not think any of the adults of the First Nations village enjoyed this music, after our peace pipe was passed around several times, I think they began to appreciate it a little bit more. The more they smoked, the happier they became. I must tell you, there is nothing funnier than seeing adults from the Cree village dressed as hippies, dancing to rock and roll music around a large fire, after they had smoked from our peace pipe. Though kids were not supposed to smoke marijuana at the festivals, Noodin, Hurit, and I had our own peace pipe, which we used on these special occasions. When the marijuana crop was harvested, I would always stash away a little bit of the crop for such special occasions.

The Cree also had many cultural ceremonies and rituals, including the Sun Dance, pow wows, vision quests, pipe ceremonies, walking-out ceremony, and sweat lodges. I participated in every ceremony I was able to, for I so loved going to their village. I would always stay in Noodin and Hurit's teepee, as their family had adopted me as an honorary member of their tribe. I loved getting dressed up and dancing around a fire to the sound of the drums. It was a glorious time, a time that would bond the three of us throughout our lives.

It would be remiss of me if I did not talk about some of the other celebrations we had at Tranquility as well. Besides the Harvest Festival, we also celebrated the Grateful Dead Day in early May. This holiday was associated with the planting of our garden each year. The Grateful Dead were my parents' favorite rock and roll band. Noodin and Hurit simply could not understand how a band that was dead could be grateful, though we always had great fun celebrating this day. We dressed up in our best hippie clothes and danced to the music of the Grateful Dead blasting over several loudspeakers all day long.

In addition to the Harvest Festival and the Grateful Dead Day, there was Woodstock Day, which took place in mid-August. This holiday was a happy, joyous day during which we celebrated world peace, love, and togetherness with, of course, classic rock and roll music, while everyone liberally shared the peace pipe and danced throughout the day.

There was also Earth Day, which is a day we celebrated and offered thanks to Mother Earth and appreciated our relationship with our planet. On Peace Day, we celebrated our desire for peace around the world, and there was also Gathering of the Tribes Day, which we celebrated in January with our Cree neighbors. Since this last holiday is in the middle of the winter, we held it in our largest log cabin that houses the school. On this day, everyone sits around talking about spirituality and the meaning of life. There are some very intense conversations on that day, especially toward the end of the day after the peace pipe has been passed around many times.

These festivals between the two villages helped strengthen the bonds between us and our Cree neighbors. As I got older and the years passed, my own feelings began to evolve; I started to fall in love with Noodin. I missed him so much when we were not together and thought about him every day; he told me he felt the same way. Many years later, after I had left and returned to

Tranquility, we did finally get married and consummate our union. But I will write much more about that later in my story.

How Life is Meant to be Lived?

All who are struggling must be recognized, helped, and cared for. All resources on planet must be equally shared. There should not be hunger, homelessness, climate change, war, poverty, religious conflict, or any of the many other isolating self-centered problems plaguing the world.

We may rid ourselves of these problems now. All we lack is the will to do so. Selflessly helping each other, regardless of our differences, in times of need, is how life is meant to be lived. Only then may our hearts soften, allowing us to truly understand the reason we were born.

Chapter 8:
Life at 16 Years Old

hen I turned sixteen I was considered an adult. At this age, the children in Tranquility moved out of their parent's house and into a dormitory type home, where we would all live together. There were a few older adults living there as well to keep an eye on us, though we decided the rules of the house and what we must do so we all can live together in peace and harmony as a group. By this age, we knew all about life; at least we thought we did. We understood not only what was important so we all could survive, but also the importance of sharing, helping, and treating each other with understanding and thoughtfulness.

I could not wait to move into the teenage dormitory. It was a sign I was finally an adult and ready to be independent. By this time, Noodin and I were a couple. I loved him dearly, as I knew he loved me. We had known each other forever and spent many hours talking and holding each other. We were so happy when we were together, holding hands and enjoying life. Though we were brought up differently, our fundamental beliefs were really quite similar. I knew we were destined to be together.

As part of the First Nations tribe, Noodin believed, as I did, in the sanctity of all life and of Mother Earth. I found the teachings of the First Nations tribe fascinating and enjoyed attending many ceremonies and rituals in their village throughout the years. Nothing was ever taken for granted or not appreciated. When they would hunt for animals, they always offered thanks to the spirit of the animal for their sacrifice. They also used every part of the animal for food, clothing, making blankets or to make crafts, which they would then trade with us for things we had made or bought in Banff. Though our two villages were quite different, there were many similarities as well: the respect for life, each other, and Mother Earth binding us together as one.

Now that I was considered an adult, I had more freedom to explore and do things unsupervised. Noodin, Hurit, and I spent quite a lot of time with each other during the next five years, enjoying each other's company and learning about and sharing each other's culture more fully.

While I easily fit in and accepted the beliefs of their village, I think the culture shock Noodin and Hurit experienced was far more profound than mine. Can you imagine immersing yourself in a village such as Tranquility, which is based on spirituality and love? Though the hippie culture ended many years ago, life in Tranquility appeared to be stuck in a time warp, where the beliefs of the 1960s and 70s culture remained a permanent reality. The result of living and being brought up here was extraordinary though. Imagine living in a world where humility, empathy, selflessness, and love dominate every life; where fear, hate, and loneliness do not exist, and where every life is treated as unique and important. If only these enlightened beliefs existed in the world today, so many of the problems I saw during my travels, possibly would no longer exist.

The day I turned sixteen and moved into the dormitory, I was very excited. All the kids knew each other since we had grown up together. All the petty disagreements seen elsewhere did not exist here. No one spoke ill of another; this was simply never done. We all wanted everyone to succeed in life; we have always been taught success in life can only be achieved when we all succeed together. Success is never an individual achievement, rather it is a collective effort.

We were brought up to understand the answers to living a meaningful life could only be found within each of us, where the spirit exists and may never be found elsewhere. By seeking happiness through money, possessions, or anything else found in the world, only struggle, depression, and anxiety may result. Following the spiritual path within, as we were all encouraged to do, however, will lead to inner peace and contentment instead.

At this time in my life, I began to reevaluate some of the things I was brought up to believe. It was not that I did not believe them, I had just never been exposed to anyone who believed anything else. I was brought up in a village where consideration for everyone in the community was more important than being concerned only for oneself. Children learned at a very young age negative behaviors and selfishness were not acceptable; if they acted out, they would gently be reminded otherwise by anyone in the village. There were no tantrums or yelling. Instead, the good in everyone and everything alive was always reinforced. Positive qualities were emphasized, while negative qualities, such as hate, fear, anger, and prejudice, were discouraged.

Children were brought up to live their life with awe and wonder and to embrace the many possibilities life has to offer, rather than harbor fear about what may happen to them. Though we were taught to fear some animals that may hurt us or situations where we may be put in danger, we were always encouraged not to be afraid of life. The opposite was encouraged; we were taught to welcome life instead. By the time we started school, at five years old, these values were deeply ingrained in each of us, and they were to direct us, in a very positive way, for the rest of our life.

View Life With Awe and Wonder

What is learned during the first five years of a child's life, may affect the rest of their life. The many struggles we have throughout our lives often result from the beliefs we developed during these early, impressionable years, and the acceptance of the many false self-centered messages we learned and believed to be true, as we were taught how to survive in a self-centered world.

During these years if a child is taught to view the world and others through a dark negative prism, one where fear and worry for yourself, dominate love and concern for the well-being of others, the challenges these children will face will be the source of stress, anxiety, and endless worry.

If, however, during these early years, they instead embrace love over fear, learn to be genuinely concerned for the success and happiness of everyone rather than only for themselves, Their lives will take a much different direction. These children will learn to view life with awe and wonder, rather than with fear and distrust.

Chapter 9:
Exploring the World

A
fter living with the other kids for five years, I had a burning desire to see what life was like elsewhere. Except for the trips we took to Banff during the summer months and our visits to the Cree village near us, I had never seen the outside world. You could say I was brought up in a bubble, isolated, and I had a need, a yearning, to meet other people and see what life was really like elsewhere.

In school, we learned how big the world was and I knew there was so much to see and do. I could not wait to experience it; therefore, at the age of 21, I packed up my few possessions in a backpack and, on one of the trips we took to Banff, I simply remained behind when everyone returned to Tranquility. It was the start of a two-year long adventure that opened my eyes to the realities of what living in the world was really like. What I was to see was quite different from what I had expected. Everyone was happy and content in Tranquility and the Cree village, yet what I saw, after I left the security and safety of both, was such loneliness and unhappiness my heart ached.

Where I was raised, no one was alone or unloved. Yet, outside our small town, this was not the case. Everywhere else, there appeared to be many who lived in fear, lonely, struggling trying to survive the day. Though I knew these emotions existed, I was surprised they were so prevalent. I could not understand how or why anyone would choose to live this way.

I left Tranquility on a warm early summer's day in 1993, hitching a ride into Banff with my father during the weekly farmers' market. During a previous visit to Banff, I had already made arrangements with one of the local merchants to work at their souvenir shop in the town. As part of my pay, they allowed me to sleep in a small storage room at the back of the shop. I bought a hot plate with my first paycheck so I could have cooked meals as well. I really had everything I needed, and I was excited to start my adventure.

I worked in Banff through late fall when the number of tourists began to decrease. By then, I had saved up a few thousand dollars and was ready to see the world. Since I was born in Canada, I was a Canadian citizen and obtained my passport before my trip began. Though my parents and many others told me how harsh and mean the world was, I had to see it myself. So, after the tourist season ended, on a cool fall day in late October, I packed up my belongings, left my job at the souvenir shop, and bought a bus ticket to New York City.

The reason I chose this destination was because my father was born in New York; his brother lived in Manhattan and had an apartment there. He was delighted to hear I wanted to come to New York and told me I could stay with him as long as I wanted and sleep in the spare room of his apartment. He was even going to pick me up at the bus station, so all the arrangements were made.

New York City was only to be the first stop of my trip; I ended up staying there almost a whole year. There was so much to see and do, and though I thought I knew what to expect, I was to find out I really did not know anything. I was absolutely shocked at what life was really like outside Tranquility.

My bus arrived at Grand Central Station in Manhattan on a cloudy, cold rainy day on Halloween, the last day of October. My uncle met me when the bus arrived and, though I had never met him before, he looked so much like my father I recognized him immediately. I was excited to be there, yet I must admit the noise and sheer number of people at the terminal was quite overwhelming. Banff was the only city I had previously seen and there were only about 8,000 people who lived there. Yet here, there seemed to be almost as many people crowded just into this bus station as there were in the entire city of Banff.

We took a city bus to his apartment in Manhattan. My uncle lived in a small two-bedroom apartment, which overlooked the crowded street below. Over the next year, I would spend many hours looking out the window at all the people walking by. I was fascinated not only by the sheer number of people, but also by how different they all looked. There were people of all colors, shapes, and sizes, who simply walked by without greeting or even looking at each other. In Tranquility, everyone greeted each other with a smile and hug, and they sincerely cared about how you were doing. Nothing could have prepared me for what I was to see and learn during the year I spent in New York City, especially the isolation, loneliness, and uncaring attitude of many of its residents.

The day after I arrived in New York, once my uncle left for work, I decided to take a walk to see what life was like in Manhattan. I was amazed at how many people there were on the streets and all the noise in the city. In Tranquility, not only was it mostly quiet, but there were only about 500 people who lived there. I spent much of the day walking, looking at not only the tall buildings of the city, but also at the thousands of people I walked past. Many of them were dressed in nice suits and dresses, but there were also those who were sitting and leaning against buildings, dressed in tattered clothing. Many of them were holding signs and held their hands out, asking the strangers who passed by them for money. Only a few stopped, however, to help these unfortunate souls or even look at them. It was cold on this day and some of those who I passed were not even wearing a warm coat, socks, or shoes. I did not understand why any of this needed to happen; no one was ever ignored or left unaided if they needed anything in Tranquility.

Everyone appeared to be strangers; no one talked to each other. They simply walked past one another, not smiling, or acknowledging the others' presence. They all seemed to be lonely and sad as they aimlessly ignored each other, lost in an uncaring world. My uncle had tried to warn me about what life was like in New York City, but until I saw it for myself, I simply could not understand people could treat each other this way.

As I walked by thousands of people on my first day out in New York, a few things especially caught my attention. First, it was how alone everyone appeared to be. People were rushing past each other, ignoring everyone else. They each isolated themselves in their own cocoon, surrounded shoulder to shoulder by people, yet totally alone. They rushed by to reach their destination, with an empty vacant stare in their eyes, ignoring the realities of life surrounding them. They not only passed each other, but also walked by many others who were homeless, cold, or asking for help, so they could buy something to eat or a coat and pair of socks to try to stay warm. Almost no one acknowledged any of these unfortunate people were present, or offered to help them; instead, they stared straight ahead, making themselves believe they did not even exist.

Many people also appeared angry, hateful, or fearful. The few exchanges I overheard were people yelling at others for things as absurd as the fact they looked different. They hated and feared others because the color of their skin was different, had different religious beliefs, or were dressed in tattered or provocative clothing.

I felt as if I was living in an alternate universe, one where concern for oneself replaced concern for others, hate replaced love, and fear replaced trust and hope. It was a world I did not recognize or had ever seen before. As I was to find out during the next two years, these beliefs and attitudes also existed in every part of the world. I finally came to understand it was not everyone in the world who was living in an alternate universe; rather, it was I and everyone who lived in Tranquility and the Cree village who were living in an alternative world instead. The values, beliefs, and norms of respect, caring, compassion, selflessness, and love I grew up accepting without question did not appear to exist in other places outside the idyllic village I grew up in.

This is not what life is supposed to be like. By the time I had returned that evening to my uncle's apartment, I was totally disillusioned. I had left Tranquility to see what life was really like and what I saw that first day left me shaken to my core. I was determined though, to find the good every person inherently has for each other. The rest of the year I continued searching New York for these innate qualities I believed we all possess. What follows will describe my search and what I learned.

Within a few days, my uncle and I developed a daily routine. My uncle worked a lot, and after he departed for work each day, I would leave his apartment to further explore the city. I felt terrible for many of those I saw; the sadness and loneliness in their eyes was something I had never seen in another person before I left Tranquility. I often would come home in the evening with tears in my eyes and was comforted by my uncle, as he tried to help me understand the helplessness I felt when I saw others in need.

I wanted to feel useful and try to do something to improve the lives of those who were struggling. The first week I was there, I found a soup kitchen about two miles from where my uncle lived. I went in to ask if there was anything I could do to help. They were very glad to include me as a volunteer, both cooking and serving food to those in need, who did not even have enough money to buy a meal to eat. Many of these same people were unable to afford an apartment to live in and were, therefore, homeless as well, living on the streets of New York City. I also spent time volunteering at a nearby church, where many of the homeless slept on the pews on the cold winter nights.

Most of next year I was either at the soup kitchen or at the church where the homeless were sheltered, trying in any way I could to help those who were not as fortunate as I. While I was there, I met many different people from all over the world. Though I had read and learned about different cultures in school, it was not until I experienced being there, I gained a true appreciation of how different we all are. There were many teenagers, as well as older adults among those who were hungry and homeless. Though I felt bad for everyone who was homeless and hungry, the saddest of those I saw were single mothers who, with their young children, were forced to live like this. Seeing these young, vulnerable, innocent children cold, hungry, and afraid tested how much I could bear.

There were also people of all religions, ethnicities, and races who somehow ended up on the streets, struggling each day to survive. The one thing they all had in common was life had been difficult for them. Some were mentally ill, while others became homeless for other reasons. They deserved to be treated better than this; instead, they were being ignored by society.

I wondered how humanity could allow this to happen. In Tranquility, we were brought up to believe every life is special, sacred, and equal and should be treated as such. To see such tragedy in the hearts and souls of the many I met caused me much sorrow. I struggled to understand the inhumanity I was seeing, but was never able to fully understand how any of this could be allowed to happen in a loving, caring society.

Many of the teenagers I met, as well as women my age, became prostitutes, having sex with many others every day just to make enough money to buy daily necessities. I was horrified to see the degradation of their bodies and spirit; they often finished their day with bruises, crying because of the horror they felt in having to demean themselves every day.

I met and talked to many people over the next year, hearing stories of how different circumstances in their life led them to become homeless. I talked to many veterans, who had served their country in different wars. The experiences they had during the war often left them with emotional problems so severe they could not effectively function in society. They ended up getting divorced, being unable to keep a job or pay their bills, and therefore, they too joined the ranks of the hungry and homeless.

Many of the teenagers, who I met at the soup kitchen and homeless shelter, ran away from abusive homes, where their parents were either alcoholics or strung out on drugs. Some were even sexually abused and raped by their parent or a close relative. They, therefore, chose to leave their homes and travel to New York City, hoping to begin a new life there.

Some of those on the streets were just children, as young as nine or ten years old. Many of them were living in foster homes because their parents had either died or were unable to take care of them. As I was to find out, some foster homes neglected and treated many of the children with contempt and abuse. They therefore decided to leave these homes and, having no family to return to, were forced to learn how to survive on their own.

I also met many people who suffered from bad luck or tragedy in their life, causing them to lose everything and become homeless as well. Some lost their jobs, got divorced, became sick, or witnessed a life changing event pushing their lives in a new direction. This could happen to any of us at any time. As others looked with disgust at them, I do not believe they realized if their own circumstances changed, it could be them or someone they love who ended up living like this as well.

I, therefore, spent the majority of the next year trying to help those less fortunate than I was. I knew I always had a loving family to return to, which consisted of not only my parents, but everyone who lived in our village as well. I also had a place to live while I was staying in New York, so I did not have to worry about being homeless or hungry. Those who I tried to help though, were not as lucky as I was. They were mostly ignored by others, who walked by these less fortunate souls, totally ignoring them as if their lives were worthless and unimportant.

I knew, as did everyone in Tranquility, no one's life was worthless or unimportant. Every life is sacred, equal, and deserving to be treated with respect and love. No one is better or more important than another, regardless of their skin color, job, wealth, beliefs, or anything else used by society to differentiate and judge people. We are all on the same journey of rediscovery, trying to return to the spiritual path we are all meant to pursue, rather than the self-centered path of the ego we are taught will lead to success and happiness. In Tranquility, though what we learn to survive and get along with others is part of us, its influence is minimal. The focus throughout our lives is to pursue the spiritual path by selflessly sharing our unconditional love with all others.

During the two years I spent away from home, I discovered most of the world ended up following the misguided self-centered path through life instead. This false path leads to most of the vast problems society faces today and has faced throughout history. Those living this way struggle every day to find true happiness and inner peace, looking for answers in the world around them, rather than looking to the spiritual path within, where the answers we all seek have always been.

When I was growing up, during our many spiritual discussions, I learned all living things are born with a spirit within. The spirit represents the true path we are meant to take during our lives. If we follow this path, our lives will be meaningful and full of love.

When I was not volunteering at the soup kitchen or the homeless shelter, I spent several evenings a week singing and playing guitar in a few different coffee houses in Greenwich Village, a hippie enclave in New York City. I had become quite good playing guitar and singing through the years and thought this would be a good way to make some new friends and earn some money. I would often take to the stage and sing many of the classic rock and roll and folk songs I had learned growing up. Though I did not know any current music from the 80s and 90s, it appeared everyone enjoyed the same music I did. I played songs sung by Janis Joplin, the Rolling Stones, and Led Zeppelin, as well as many folk songs from all my favorite artists. I loved being on stage just sitting on a stool, playing my guitar, and singing. From the reception I got from the audience, I think my music was well received. The owners of the coffee houses noticed more people came when I was performing. They therefore began to pay me each night I sang. By the time I left New York City, I had saved up almost $5,000 from performing. This money would sustain me for the next part of my journey.

I did meet many other artists during these nights and joined a few of them, jamming, and singing duets together. I even met a few famous singers, though to my surprise, they were not as I had expected them to be. Though they sung about love and nature, their demeanor was just like everyone else I met since I had first arrived in New York City. They seemed distant and artificial, not fully committed to sharing their love unconditionally with others. I had placed all these artists on a pedestal, thinking they made such beautiful music because they must be extraordinary people. Though I am sure some of them are, the ones I met simply blended into the crowd with everyone else.

I also spent a lot of time reading and learning what living in the rest of the world is like. I learned about people dying from war, drugs, starvation, treatable illnesses, and so much more. I read about how Mother Earth was being mistreated, how pollution and global warming are destroying our air, land, and water and may lead to the end of all life on our planet. I also learned about the mistreatment of many animals, to the point where many species are becoming extinct.

The main thing I discovered though, during my time away from Tranquility, were the dominant emotions I saw were fear and selfishness. Concern only for oneself, rather than for everyone else, dictated how everyone's lives were being lived. If only everyone could be selfless, share, have empathy and respect for each other and Mother Earth, life on our planet could finally evolve, ending the needless struggles of so many. I know this is possible because I grew up this way. I only hope there will be others who will join me, wishing to improve life on our planet before it is too late.

I never could understand though, while there were people as far as the eye could see in every direction, hardly anyone talked to or even acknowledged others. They simply walked quickly past each other, ignoring everyone they passed. No one ever smiled, seemed happy, or stopped to say hello. Those people who were less fortunate were ignored. When they asked others for help, they briskly walked by them, not even acknowledging they were there or in need. Many who were homeless appeared cold, hungry, weak, often having a blank, dazed look in their eyes telling of their hardships. During my year in New York, I went out of my way to talk to everyone I could.

There was no religion in Tranquility, rather there was simply a belief in spirituality. As I was to find out, religion and spirituality are two very different things. It was difficult for me to understand how the formal religions I saw in New York City and around the world appeared to separate, rather than unite people. Though almost all religions believe in god, many looked down on others who may have believed differently than them. Whether you believed in Christianity, Judaism, Islam, Buddhism, Hinduism, or any of the many other religions practiced around the world, religion should not divide people. I read about the war in Northern Ireland, where Catholics and Protestants were killing each other. In the Middle East, it was the Muslims and Jews who were often at war. In South and Southeast Asia, Hindus, Buddhists, and Muslims killed each other. All of these and other wars were simply the result of believing differently in god.

It did not make sense to me. We are all equal, the same. No one religion is better or superior to another. I believe in god, though my belief is that god, spirit, soul, exists within me and within all living things. Though organized religion may have started out with altruistic goals, it appears to have lost its way. Instead of religious tenets being dictated by the spirit within us, it has allowed itself to be dominated by what we learned and were socialized to believe instead. I was raised to believe every single life has purpose and meaning. If religion divides us and causes people to hate, be afraid of, and kill each other because of their differences, maybe it is time to reevaluate the role religion has in the world today. Perhaps it is time for a spiritual revolution, one where the spirit dictates how we treat each other, rather than our different beliefs in god.

In Tranquility, we are taught to meditate from a very young age and to listen to our spirit, understanding all the questions we have about life will be answered if we follow our spirit's loving path through life. It is only after we are born, socialized, and exposed to the many experiences' life presents us, our understanding about life becomes distorted and confused. We forget that love, understanding, compassion, and empathy are our inherent qualities, and hate, fear, and selfishness only result from accepting the false self-centered ideas and beliefs we learn after we are born.

The reason we are alive, the meaning of life, is to listen quietly to the spirit within and follow the path it leads you on. The spirit is pure and only becomes disoriented when we believe what we are taught, instead of what we inherently know to be true. After we are born, what we learn will often encourage us to follow a false path through life. Though some of what we learn is important and will help us survive in the world, it will not bring contentment, inner peace, understanding, and knowledge about life's true purpose that so many desire.

In the world, money, prestige, material possessions, and everything else we are taught defines success is considered important. It is believed if you possess all these things, your life will be successful, and you will be happy. It appears, after observing and meeting many others during my two years away from Tranquility, almost everyone has bought into this illusion society has told them. The exact opposite is true though. None of these things actually define true success or bring happiness. Success and happiness may only truly be found within by following the guidance of the spirit, then they must be shared with all others. It may not be found in a self-centered world or anywhere else.

Several months before I left New York City, I wrote a letter to Hurit. I asked her if she wanted to join me on a walkabout; this was something we had talked about many times since we first heard about it from Bear. Like me, Hurit also had a burning desire to see the world, and she readily agreed. We planned to meet in New York City in the fall and begin our trip.

To make the money needed for this, Hurit told me she would talk to the owner of the souvenir shop in Banff, where I had worked the previous year. If he would hire her, she would save all the money she made for our journey. Luckily, the owner of the shop was very happy to have her work there and would let her sleep in the small room behind the shop, just as I had. By the time fall came and tourist season was drawing to a close, Hurit had saved several thousand dollars and was ready to join me for our adventure.

We are All Equal, Important, and Connected

It does not matter what job you have, how much money you make, the color of your skin, your ethnicity, religious preference, or any other comparison we may make. We are all equal, important, and connected.

Only when everyone succeeds in life, regardless of our differences, will our lives truly have meaning.

Chapter 10:
Walkabout

A fter my year in New York City, though I was quite disillusioned with what I had seen, I still desired to see what life was like in other parts of the world. So, on a cool fall day in October 1994, Hurit took a bus from Banff to New York City and, just as my uncle had met me almost a year ago, I met her at Grand Central Station. Using part of our savings, we each had bought a good backpack and filled it with all the necessities we would need. We had also decided the first stop on our walkabout would be Calcutta, India.

A few months before our trip was to begin, we each bought a plane ticket to Calcutta and got a work visa allowing us to work in India. The reason we chose Calcutta is we hoped to volunteer at one of Mother Teresa's charitable homes. With our backpacks filled and work visa and passport in hand, we boarded a shuttle taking us from Grand Central Station to LaGuardia Airport, where we then boarded a plane marking the beginning of our walkabout.

Neither of us had ever been on an airplane before and we were quite excited. It was a very long flight, taking over 15 hours in total. Since we had not seen each other for almost a year, we talked almost the entire trip. Hurit told me everything going on in her village and what she knew was happening in Tranquility. We also naively talked about helping those less fortunate than us by volunteering to help the sick and poor in India. Since I had spent almost one year in New York City, I thought I was prepared to handle the challenges awaiting me. In reality, nothing could have been further from the truth. After we landed in India, we took a taxi to Sudder Street, where we stayed in a hostel during our time in Calcutta.

I will never forget this taxi ride; it was our first look at what life in another country on the other side of the world was like. The dusty, noisy streets were filled with people sleeping on the side of the road, while others searched through the garbage, hoping to find something to eat. There were children being bathed in puddles by their mothers and families sleeping exposed to the elements. There were children begging, dressed in tattered rags that were supposed to protect them from the cool weather. Never could I have imagined anyone would allow others to live like this. I cannot describe the sheer helplessness we felt as our taxi drove past them.

That evening we settled into the hostel, and the next morning, we went to orientation for those who wanted to volunteer in one of Mother Teresa's homes. We were told those we would care for were the unwanted, forgotten, sick, disabled, and who were living on the margins of society. We were given a choice of which home we wanted to volunteer at; we chose to volunteer at Mother Teresa's Home for the Dying.

Since we saw many people die while we were at the Home for the Dying, this would be a good time to talk about our beliefs about death. We had many lively discussions about this. Death was not feared in Tranquility; it was believed to simply be an extension of our journey through life. We believe the self or ego, which comes into existence when we are born, dies when the body does. The spirit, however, which is within everything alive, is eternal, and returns to a different plane of existence at a higher vibrational level, one where it joins other spirits in an ambience of unconditional love. Therefore, it is our belief death is not the end, rather it represents a new beginning. Also, we believe the spirit of the person or any life who died, though no longer here, continues to live on in the hearts and spirit of those it met and influenced during its life.

I think the best example of this was when Rocky, my pet racoon, died. Though he had a long, happy life and physically was no longer alive, his spirit will remain and live in my heart forever. The same is true for every life. Knowing this, we knew our spirit would continue past physical death, both in the hearts and spirit of those we loved and helped during our life, as well as on an ethereal plane, where it would live forever with others like it. We therefore did not fear death; rather we embraced it as an extension of our eternal journey of life.

During those two months, rarely was there a day without at least one person passing away. Most of those who were at the home were alone, in pain, and often afraid. We did our best to comfort them and be there with them as their spirit prepared to return home. Though the volunteer work was emotionally and physically exhausting, it was also extraordinarily rewarding.

We worked long hours, spending four hours each morning and three hours every afternoon six days a week, feeding, bathing, and anything else asked of us, trying our best to help in any way we could. It was my belief every single person's life had meaning, was important, and deserved to be cared for and loved; every life was equally important. I spent many hours sitting at the bedside of those dying, holding their hand. No one should have to die alone, unloved. Though we could not communicate verbally with each other, words were not necessary.

We decided to remain in India a while longer after we finished our two months volunteering at Mother Teresa's Home for the Dying. I was quite interested in learning more about different religious beliefs, since religion appeared to have such a large influence on many people in the world. As centers for two of the major religions of the world, Buddhism and Hinduism, we decided to visit temples of each in India to learn more about them.

We learned Buddhism began around 500 BC and is based on the teachings of Siddhartha Gautama. After sitting under an ancient Bodhi tree, he attained enlightenment and became known as Lord Buddha. The basic beliefs, as I understand them, state the world is suffering, suffering has a cause, and you can end suffering. To do so, you must follow the enlightened path, which is a set of guidelines for behaving properly. To reach enlightenment, one must have wisdom, compassion, kindness, and love for all life.

Hinduism believes in the continuous cycle of life, death, and reincarnation. They believe all living creatures have a soul which is eternal and part of the Supreme Soul. Reincarnation occurs when the ego or self dominates the soul or spirit during life; this makes the soul impure. If the soul is impure when it dies, it will be reincarnated into a new life, only to repeat the cycle again.

Though these are very simplistic explanations for these two religions, I found some of their underlying beliefs interesting and even similar to some of the beliefs I grew up with. I too believe in an eternal soul, which is part of the Supreme Soul. Since I believe everything alive has a spirit, a piece of god within them, then together we are all part of a Supreme Soul. Remember, in Tranquility, there is no difference between the concepts of god, soul, and spirit; we consider all three to be the same.

As I have come to understand from my study of many different religious beliefs, an awakening is when there is a realization there is a spirit within every living thing. Enlightenment is simply the complete acceptance of this. When one becomes enlightened, though the ego will always remain with each of us throughout our lives, it no longer dominates our thoughts and actions. Rather, the spirit becomes our primary decision maker. And with enlightenment comes a genuine understanding about our purpose in life.

It would be careless of me, before moving on to talk about the rest of our journey, if I did not discuss the caste system in India. Though discrimination based on the caste system is illegal, it still has a profound influence on Indian society. There still, to this day, remains caste abuse and segregation as a result of this illegal system. In general, there are five social classes or castes in Indian society. First, there are the Brahmins, which is the highest class and includes priests or scholars. Below them are the Kshatriyas, the nobles and warriors, the Vaishyas, who conduct business, the Shudras, who are the laborers or servants, and finally, the Untouchables, who do undesirable jobs like cleaning sewers.

What I found so interesting is the parallels this system shares with those found in my home country of Canada and other countries in the world. In Canada, though there is no caste system, the First Nations tribes and other minorities are treated as inferior to the dominant majority, composed primarily of the white class; similarly, they too often work menial jobs. This also appears to be true in many countries, be it the minority non-white ethnicities in the United States, the Aboriginal tribes of Australia, or the pre-apartheid treatment of black people in South Africa. I was raised to believe all life, regardless of race, religion, wealth, beliefs, sex, and any other comparison made, is equal and precious. No one is better or more important than another. Could this be the reason there are so many problems and hardships experienced by so many throughout the world? Has the world accepted this self-ish egoistic view of life?

Due to the many stories we had heard from Bear, after we left India, Hurit and I wanted to meet the Aboriginals in the Australian Outback. He had hoped we would stop by his village during our walkabout, so we could tell his family how he was doing. Bear's village was called Wiluna, which was located in Western Australia. He had written a letter to his brother, which my father mailed from Banff, to let him know we were his good mates and might stop by to visit. We, therefore, contacted Bear's brother before we left India. He was very happy to hear from us and invited us to stay with him and his family while we were there.

Consequently, in January of 1995, our backpacks replenished with fresh supplies, we flew to the small airport in Wiluna, where Bear's brother met us upon our arrival. During our visit, we were to learn a lot from Bear's family, including their history and what life for the Aboriginal people was really like.

Wiluna is located in the Outback and is an Aboriginal Australian village with a population of about 500, similar to that of Tranquility. It is surrounded by desert landscape stretching endlessly in every direction; it takes over a day to get to the nearest city. Unlike Tranquility, which was located in the cool Rocky Mountains, the weather in Wiluna ranged from a low in the mid-20s at night, to a high in the 120's during the day. The roads leading to Wiluna were poorly maintained, and many local animals and insects, including snakes, lizards, spiders, tarantulas, dingoes, camels, kangaroos, and many other critters, shared the Outback with the village.

The history of the Aboriginal people was very interesting. They first arrived by sea from Southeast Asia, almost 50,000 years ago, long before the arrival of the first colonists. As we were to discover, there were many similarities between the First Nations tribes in Canada and the Aboriginals in Australia. In fact, the parallels between the two cultures, separated by many thousands of miles and an ocean, were eerily similar. They were both exploited by Europeans, to the great harm of their culture and people. The English first arrived and began to colonize Australia in 1788; the European definition of the word colonize is to take over or lay claim to, which is exactly what they did. The Indigenous peoples of both countries were considered second class citizens, living in poverty and given poor access to both education and healthcare.

Many Aboriginal communities were located in small, isolated towns like Wiluna, in unwanted desert areas of Australia. The Aboriginal people were originally mostly nomadic hunter-gatherers, much like the First Nations tribes in Canada. In the twentieth century, government policies forced almost a third of Aboriginal Australian children to be forcibly removed from their homes. These were known as the stolen generations. They were then often put in institutions, where they were encouraged to forget about their culture and accept the values and beliefs of the dominant white society instead; they were also forbidden from speaking their own language.

These institutions reminded me of stories the Elders of Hurit's village would tell us about the abuse and suffering so many First Nations children experienced when they were forced to leave their homes in the late 1800s and early 1900s. The Elders told us over 100,000 First Nations children were removed from their families and forcibly sent to residential schools to be reeducated.

I could go on about the many similar cruel harsh things done to both communities, though, as I was to find out during my two years away from Tranquility, this callousness and disregard for other cultures and the lives of other Indigenous people extended to many other countries around the world as well.

In North America, especially in the United States, not only were black people enslaved, but even after they were freed, they still suffered tremendous prejudice and inequality continuing to this day. In addition to black people, Hispanic, Asian, Native American people and basically anyone who was not white, were discriminated against as well.

When we travelled to Africa upon leaving Wiluna, we learned of a policy of racism, discrimination, and segregation called apartheid in South Africa. This policy allowed the minority white population to rule unfairly in South Africa, despite the fact almost three quarters of the population was black and only 13% was white; apartheid actually ended in 1994, the year we were in Africa.

When we later travelled to the United States, Central, and South America, we learned about the genocide of Indigenous peoples, especially by the British and Spanish empires in all of the Americas. From the time white Europeans first arrived in the Americas in the 1400s, almost 90% of the Indigenous population vanished within the first 200 years, falling from about 145 million people to 15 million. They died of disease, especially smallpox, measles, and cholera, as well as due to the indiscriminate killing of men, women, and children by the superior white Europeans.

As we had learned while we were in India, the Indian people also suffered; millions died as a result of British colonial rule and their subsequent genocide of the Indian people. In all these places, the systematic culling of Indigenous cultures and populations, due to the greed and avarice of white Europeans who felt they were superior to the native populations, was not uncommon.

Before we were to head home, we briefly visited several countries in Europe. Though each country we visited was different, the one commonality we found across the globe was everyone's desire to find happiness and love. Many of the people we met in Africa and South America were quite poor; due to poverty, their thoughts were almost always on how they and their family could survive each day. They were worried about their basic needs for survival: food, shelter, water, and safety. There were wars, starvation, disease, homelessness, and much more in many of these countries. We heard of people being killed, simply because they looked or believed differently from others. Children, sometimes as young as six years old, were alone, wandering the streets trying to find food and a safe place to stay. In Brazil, it is estimated anywhere from 200,000 to 8 million children are homeless, trying to survive the many dangers and harsh living conditions no child should ever have to know.

Hunger and malnourishment were especially difficult sights for us to behold. In Africa, we saw children too small for their age, their ribs protruding from their bodies, die needlessly. These children reminded me of pictures of holocaust survivors I saw in books when I visited the library in Banff. Often, donated food was available, but rebel forces or the government prevented it from reaching those who needed it most.

Seeing people go hungry and die from starvation is senseless. We have the ability to feed everyone in the world now; we just lack the will to do so. The same is true of homelessness, treatable diseases, lack of clean water, and most other problems we witnessed and heard about during our time traveling the world. Instead of sharing needed medications with those in poor countries to eradicate treatable diseases, we would see people die needlessly because wealthier countries would not provide these medications at no or minimal costs. The greed of the few outweighed the need of the many. The fact this was acceptable was beyond our understanding.

The horrors of the world, the sadness, hatred, fear, anger, extreme poverty, war, drugs, homelessness, hunger, and selfishness of many I met and read about was opposite of what I believed life should be like and how I was brought up. The world I had just seen was full of loneliness and hardships. Life in the outside world was full of competition, where the strongest person survives and those who are the weakest or unluckiest, struggle to even get through the day. I saw so many people who were lonely, went hungry each day, were sick, depressed, or who had no place to live, being ignored by everyone around them. There were even children and families who were hungry and homeless. I will never understand how humanity could allow this to happen.

As I was to discover, just as my parents had many years ago, the world outside Tranquility was not a place I wanted to live in. The saddest lesson I learned though, is none of this was necessary. There is no reason for the struggle and hardship so many people experience during their lives. When you are brought up, as I was, to love, respect life, and to sincerely care for each other and Mother Earth, the many problems I saw need not happen. All those who are struggling, for whatever reason, must be recognized, helped, and cared for; all our resources should be equally shared. Helping each other is how life is meant to be lived. Only then may our hearts soften and may we discover the true meaning of life.

I was beginning to finally understand why my parents left the world behind, to settle in the Canadian Rocky Mountains; they viewed the world as hopeless and irredeemable. Two years ago, when I first left Tranquility, I was idealistic. I grew up sheltered and saw the world through rose-colored glasses. Now, two years later, I was beginning to understand, the world truly can be a very dark place. After being away from home for almost two years, I finally understood why my parents and their friends first moved to Tranquility 23 years ago, and why I decided it was time for me to return home as well.

The Comfort of Silence

When we see a wrong, do or say nothing, we are contributing to the decline of our world. Many have different opinions as to what is considered wrong. Spiritually, morally, and ethically, wrong is doing anything to harm another in any way. It matters not if the injury is physical, verbal, or ignoring the many human offenses we inflict on each other.

War, hunger, homelessness; prejudice, inequity, hate. These and many more human transgressions are caused by our comfort of silence, fearful of saying something to upset the status quo.

We must be silent no more. Every indiscretion must be met and challenged with resistance, speaking up loudly in defense of those being harmed. If we see anything we would not wish to happen to us or those we are closest to, that is the measure to be silent no more.

Chapter 11:
Return to Tranquility

H

urit and I returned home in the early fall of 1995, taking a plane to Banff. Once there, we stayed with the owners of the souvenir shop, where we had both worked, until the weekend, when several residents from Tranquility would come to Banff to sell their crafts to the few remaining tourists and buy a few last supplies before the winter fully set in. I returned to Tranquility and Hurit to her village on a Sunday evening, just as the first snow of the season began to fall. Everyone was happy to see me and wanted to know all about my adventures in New York City and around the world. We talked all night as they told me what was going on in the village and I told them about the many experiences and adventures I had and people I met while I was away.

The next day, I was excited to see Noodin again. So, early that morning, I traveled to the Cree village. They were happy to see me as well and Hurit and I spent much of the day sharing the many things we saw and did over the past year. As evening fell, Noodin and I were finally able to slip away and be alone. I missed him so much, as I knew he did me. We had known each other since we were babies and had been in love since we were teenagers. I think we always knew we would get married one day and spend the rest of our lives together. We talked, kissed, and laughed until the moon was high above us. Then, reluctantly, we returned to his village, and I spent the night in his family's teepee, as I had so many times before, sleeping by the warm fire burning in the middle of their home.

Noodin and I married in the spring of the following year. The wedding was held in Tranquility with the entire village coming to our big event; almost everyone from the Cree village came as well. It was quite a party, with a combination of classic rock and roll music playing from the many speakers dotting our village, as well as native Cree drums and dancing continuing well into the night. The food was also from both the Cree village and what we grew in our gardens in Tranquility. And, of course, we smoked and passed around the peace pipe, which was filled with our homegrown tobacco. I do not think the Cree people put marijuana in their pipes when they are home, but they did not seem to mind smoking it at all when they were in our village. Everyone thoroughly enjoyed themselves; it was by far the best party ever, and Noodin and I were so happy to be able to share and enjoy it with all those we love.

The guests also included many of the mountain men, including Bear, who periodically stopped by our village to trade and share their tall stories about their lives living in the wilderness. My best woman was, of course, Hurit, who I had known and grown up with since we were little girls. We had so many good times together and shared everything with each other.

I could not imagine a more perfect life and I looked forward to what the future would bring. We spent our honeymoon under a lean-to in the woods, located on the banks of the nearby river. The lean-to was isolated, surrounded by trees on all sides. It was here, on the night of our wedding, we first consummated our marriage, and, to our surprise, exactly nine months later, our first child was born.

We had talked a lot about what our life would be like after we were married. We decided we would have a home in both villages, living in a tepee in the Cree village and in a log cabin my parents would help us build when we were in Tranquility. We would equally split the time we spent in each village, taking part in all the traditional ceremonies and celebrations throughout the year. By this time, we were fluent in each other's language and were determined to ensure our children would be as well.

We were so excited when our child was born, but to be honest, I think our parents were even happier than we were. They volunteered to babysit, which for us was great, as we had the opportunity to spend some time alone with each other. They also watched our baby when we were busy doing chores, as everyone was required and expected to do each day. As the years went by, we had two more children. We spent our time living in both villages, so our children would benefit from learning the traditions from both cultures. By the time our children were five years old, they could speak and understand both English and the Cree language.

Just as I had, our children embraced everything they were taught. They adopted the traditions and met all the expectations of both villages. When they were at Tranquility, they did chores and went to school. As I had, they also helped in the garden and stacked wood in preparation for the coming winter. They too spent time learning from everyone who lived in the village. As for music, they learned to appreciate the sounds of classic rock and roll and folk music, not that they had any choice, since it was still the only music played in Tranquility.

The spiritual beliefs of Tranquility were passed down to my children as well, just as they had been passed down to me. They understood about the spirit and the need for love and respect for all life. Everyone in the village helped raise our children and, if they were acting out, they were gently redirected back onto the path of compassion, sharing, and consideration for all life. By the time our children, as all the children in Tranquility, were ready to begin school, they almost never acted out; these values were as ingrained in their DNA, as they were within mine and all those who were lucky enough to be brought up here.

One of the things we were taught very early in life was the world and your own thoughts may be viewed two ways: positively or negatively. The lens we look through to see the world will often determine the direction our life will take. If we see and view the world in a positive way, then the many possibilities the world has to offer will reveal themselves. By viewing the world this way, love, happiness, contentment, joy, and awe were sure to dominate our lives. Instead of viewing others in a competitive, uncaring, self-centered way, the goodness within each person could be viewed instead.

Children brought up in Tranquility were brought up only knowing positive values and beliefs; they knew nothing of the negativity other children absorb and internalize in the outside world. They, therefore, believed in freely helping each other and having empathy for others, rather than accepting the selfishness, prejudice, and hate, seen throughout the world, as normal. Their positive beliefs in life were learned at a very young age, and therefore, lasted throughout their lifetime.

For the six months we lived in the Cree village, our children participated in all the ceremonial events through the year. They learned about Cree culture at a very young age, as well as how to dance to the sound of drums, make crafts, wield a bow and arrow, hunt, fish, track animals, and much more. Though our children were not full-blooded Cree, they were accepted wholeheartedly by everyone in the village. After all, Noodin was their father and I had been accepted as part of the tribe since I was a little girl. Our children truly had the best of both worlds.

The town of Tranquility continued to grow; by the time my children were 16 years old and ready to move into the teenage dormitory, there were almost one thousand people living there. Nothing else changed though. The loving culture my parents and their four friends first introduced so many years ago still prevailed. The values of empathy, kindness, and compassion for all life and for Mother Earth remained the same as it was when they first came to this beautiful remote area in the Canadian Rocky Mountains so many years ago.

Many years have passed, and I am growing older. Except for the two years when I was 21 years old, I have spent my entire life in Tranquility and the Cree village. I have no regrets at all. From my earliest memories, I never questioned the spirit within or the direction my life was meant to take. I fully understood the path of the spirit is the true path of life; my life was, therefore, blessed with this knowledge from a very young age. It is nice to have someone to share your journey through life with, but truly, we all must take this journey alone and find our spiritual path ourselves. We can only do that though after we finally understand the path the ego, the self asks us to pursue is false and will lead to a life of endless struggle.

Though I too have an ego, as we all do, it does not play a major part in my life. It is my hope by sharing my story, others may find the love and inner peace I have been lucky enough to have known throughout my life and that they will then help their children find this as well.

Are You Your Brother's Keeper?

Is your life more important than another's? Should you not care, regardless of our differences, about helping everyone, allowing their life to be easier and more meaningful?

If you live your life in fear, concerned only for your own survival and happiness, your answer to the above questions is yes. And though you may survive, be successful, and live to an old age, your life will lack meaning.

If, however, the answer to the above questions is no, then, though you may not be as successful or live as long as others who live their life in fear, your life will be important, meaningful, and you will have learned the lesson we are alive to understand.

Chapter 12:
Many Years Later

M any years have passed since Noodin and I got married. As we approach the twilight of our lives, we are now considered Elders in the First Nations village. Our three children have grown up, and we have six grandchildren and ten great grandchildren. We still live in the Canadian Rocky Mountains, continuing to split our time living in Tranquility and the Cree village.

As I approach the end of my life, I find myself reflecting on how my life has been lived. I look back at all the experiences I had growing up living in Tranquility and the Cree village and the two years I spent away from my home. Noodin and I married shortly after I returned from my trip and our marriage has been wonderful. We raised our three children with the best traditions of both villages and, as a result, their lives were enriched. When they were older, they also passed these values on to their children. Though we prepared our children and taught them about the world outside our two villages, in case they chose to leave one day, they never did. They decided to stay and continue to live in Tranquility and the Cree village after they were older, teaching their own children the traditions they themselves had learned when they were growing up.

Today, as I sit on the porch of my log cabin and reminisce, I feel very philosophical. I look back on my life with an outlook you can only have when you are preparing to die. I remember, as I was growing up, the many debates and discussions we had almost every day in Tranquility and the Cree village about the meaning of life. Everyone in both villages helped shape my view of the world, and during those years, I learned and internalized many of the philosophies and beliefs of the residents. These debates were often very lively; everyone held an opinion they wanted to share. It was during this time the direction of my life was to take shape, as I chose to follow the spiritual path for the remainder of my life.

Now, my body has become frail; I am unable to do the things I used to do. I spend most of my time remembering my life and reflecting about life in general. The time you have left as you approach death is an interesting period in your life. So many things once appearing to be important no longer remain so. You begin to realize life really is not complicated or complex; rather, it is quite simple. The money, material possessions, job you had, and almost everything else you once thought defined what a successful life is, no longer matter.

You finally realize none of those things are important, or ever were. Rather, your life will be defined by the path you followed; specifically, whether you followed the meaningful advice and direction of your spirit or you followed the flawed path the ego wanted you to pursue instead. If you followed the former, your journey through life will have been meaningful and your life worthwhile. If, however, you followed the path of the ego, you may find you have many regrets as you prepare to die.

In Tranquility, I was brought up to believe in reincarnation and in a spiritual plane of existence, where the spirit exists, with others like it, if it has completed its human experience successfully. I found this was quite similar to the Hindu ideas I learned about during my time in India. According to the Hindu beliefs, if we do not learn the lessons we are alive to understand, our spirit will be reborn into another life, as many times as necessary, until these lessons are fully realized. If, however, we are able to learn these lessons, then our spirit joins others who have also done so on another spiritual plane. If there is a definition of god, then god is a plane of existence where all enlightened spirits throughout time exist together as one with unconditional love.

When I was in school, I learned about nature vs. nurture. How much of who we are, how we act, and what we believe is a result of our inherited genes compared to what we have learned since we were born. After growing up in Tranquility and spending two years on several continents around the world, I now realize how much influence nurture has on our lives. Everything I learned during my time away shattered my existing views of the world and those who live in it. I began to realize the degree to which nurture affects our happiness and view of the world.

I also learned the beliefs the ego will have us accept as real are a myth. I met many people who appeared to have everything yet were far from happy. Even if they were successful, they often worried about other things. The anxiety, especially from having to work in high-stress jobs to make a lot of money, appeared to cause them many psychological and physical problems.

I often wondered how someone who followed all the rules growing up, conformed to what they were taught, and became successful could be so unhappy. They did everything they were told, did well in school, made a lot of money, owned nice possessions, and had a family. Yet clearly something was missing. They were, in fact, often depressed and anxious.

Some of whom I met though, having very few possessions, appeared far happier, content, and at peace than those who appeared to have everything. They had very little money but found inner peace within. These people chose to find their happiness elsewhere and not conform to societies mores and definition of success.

During my time away, I would sit for hours, talking to almost everyone I met, learning not only about their life, but also about their beliefs. It was fascinating as I met people who observed many different religions, from many different cultures all over the world. I was surprised how many of those I met owned very little, though appeared to have found inner peace and happiness. There was a calm surrounding their being, an aura of contentment, that I often did not see in others around the world who were successful.

It is not too late for change, but time is clearly beginning to run out. The threat of nuclear war, starvation, climate change, and so much more must be addressed now. If we do not, Mother Earth, as we know it, may become uninhabitable. To make these changes, though, we all must first challenge the beliefs we were taught and alter the path we are following.

The Twilight of Life

As I sit on my porch on a cold winter day in the twilight of my life, I reflect on what is important in life. I look at the many struggles others, as well as I, had; hunger, homelessness, prejudice, inequity; life changing loss of job, divorce, illness, death, or any number of other challenges I have witnessed during my life.

I now understand how unnecessary many of these difficulties were. They were a result of living in a self-centered world, where we worry only about ourselves, rather than to be sincerely concerned for others who are struggling as well.

We need not face life alone. We are meant to help each other in our time of need, understanding every life, regardless of our differences, is equally important, and only together, may we mitigate the many self-inflicted problems caused by living in an egoistic world, allowing us all to survive and live a meaningful life full of inner peace, enduring love, and genuine purpose.

Chapter 13:
Final Thoughts

A
s death approaches, something interesting happens; you begin to review your life and wonder if you lived a good life. Was my life important? Meaningful? The reason I am writing this book is to share what I have learned. My life's journey taught me the importance of selflessly sharing my spirit and love with others.

When I look at the world, I wonder why? Why is there war, indiscriminate killing, starvation, hunger, homelessness, prejudice, hate, fear, selfishness, inequality, poverty, depression, anxiety, stress, unhappiness, and daily struggles that seem to never end? Why are some people who are successful in life, have a prestigious job, a lot of money and material possessions, unable to find inner peace, happiness, or meaning in their lives? And why are others who appear to have very little, truly happy and at peace?

The answers to these questions are not as difficult as you may think. Though, if you are struggling, how simple the answers are may surprise you. They have to do with how you are brought up or socialized, especially during the first five years of your life. If you are brought up to look to the world and others for your happiness, meaning, and success, and to be primarily concerned for only your well-being, you may never find the answers you seek. If, however, you are brought up with love, listening to the advice of the spirit, your vision may remain clear, and your life have meaning. The answers to life may never be found in the self-centered world; they may only be found by listening to and hearing the spirit that lies within. Once you clearly hear the messages from your spirit, you will understand sharing your unconditional love selflessly with others is life's purpose and will fulfill your life's journey.

If children are brought up to understand this, especially during their early formative years of their life, these feelings and all other positive emotions will become part of who they are, part of their essence. If, however, they are brought up, as the majority of the world is, believing the false truths about success they learn as they are growing up and the errant path through life this truth will have them follow, then many struggles will surely disrupt their life.

Though it is possible to change and find the true path in life you are meant to pursue after these early years, it is considerably more difficult to do. It is my hope by bringing our children up to know the answers I have shared with you, your children's journey through life, like the children who grew up in Tranquility, will be easier and more meaningful.

I did not realize, when I first began to write this book about my life, how important the lessons I learned were. I thought others might find my story interesting. Little did I understand, however, by comparing my upbringing to those who were brought up elsewhere, I would discover the cause of many of the problems, anxieties, and illnesses experienced throughout the world. I would also come to understand the answer to the two questions so many ask during their lifetime: Why am I alive? and What is the meaning of life?

Growing up as I did away from civilization and without all the modern conveniences so many have in society today, I embraced a unique perspective regarding life. I was taught by everyone in Tranquility and the Cree village to understand all life must be respected and to treat everyone as I myself want to be treated; positive emotions were always emphasized.

If children are brought up as I was, to believe in the goodness of life, to share selflessly, foster respect and love for all others, then there may be hope. If they are shown how to find their path and happiness in life from within, where the spirit is, the direction of our world may finally evolve to a higher spiritual plane.

I am writing this book at the twilight of my life. I possess a lifetime of experience, including the time I spent traveling the world, to help me present the lessons I learned. I believe there is much we can all do to change the destructive direction our world is propelling itself toward. To begin this process, however, it is important to begin with our children, teaching them to live their lives with love rather than hate, curiosity rather than fear, acceptance rather than prejudice, and selflessness rather than selfishness. If the next generation of children are brought up this way, then perhaps it will not be too late to change our destiny and our future.

Our Children May Change the World

The first five years of every child's life is the most important. It is during this time they learn what is expected of them and how they will react to different situations in the world.

It is also when they will develop an overall view of humanity and how to treat others. Their opinions, prejudices, beliefs, and aspirations, often begin during these early formative years, and will form the basis of how they will act and think about others, often for the rest of their life.

Let us therefore raise our children during these years to treat everyone with love, respect, and empathy, understanding every life, regardless of our differences, is equally deserving.

Author's Note:

It is my hope your understanding of awakening, enlightenment, and spirituality has been enhanced by reading 'Tranquility: A Village of Hope' - book 3 of 'The Awakening Tetralogy'. If it has, could you please take a few minutes to: "Write a Review" and recommend this book on social media and to your friends and family.

Tranquility was written to try to awaken and help others who are awakened more fully understand what enlightenment is, so their spiritual journey through life may be more fully realized.

Thank you for taking the time to read:
'Tranquility: A Village of Hope'. Please consider reading the other three books in this series as well.

I am including an addendum with an assortment of spiritual reflections that use metaphor, imagery, and spiritual insight to explore themes of awakening, enlightenment, and the human pursuit of meaning. These reflections are included in Book 2 of *Spiritual Reflections*. It is my hope you may consider reading the other book in this series as well as you further your search to discover the meaning of life.

Books by Ken Luball

The four Spiritual books in *The Awakening Tetralogy:*
Today I Am Going to Die: Choices in Life
The Spirit Guide: Journey Through Life
Tranquility: A Village of Hope
The Illusion of Happiness: Choosing Love Over Fear
A Mystical Trilogy: 'Our Search for Meaning' - a series of three books of thoughtful easily understandable spiritual reflections about awakening, enlightenment, spirituality, & the meaning of life.

****

A Spiritual Duology: '*Spiritual Reflections*' - Two books of spiritual reflections using metaphor, imagery, and spiritual insight to explore themes of awakening, enlightenment, and the human pursuit of meaning.

The first three stories in *The Awakening Tetralogy* are written in the first person, following the spiritual journey through life of a child, as they learn the lessons needed during their life to awaken and become enlightened. These books are written in an understandable, interesting, unique narrative, which is both thought-provoking and engaging.

To find links for each of these nine books please visit my website: kenluball.com[1].

---

1. http://kenluball.com/?fbclid=IwAR1ig1x0zSJBth8qgyuOPoC1Ynov26InfSRV0cUsnkz3fgAG13FFcnTPJ

0I

About Ken

Peace, Love, & Light

My name is Ken Luball ~ Spiritual ~ Seeker ~ Author ~ Guide ~

****

Ever since I was a young child, I knew my purpose in life; it was for me to awaken, find enlightenment, and share my experience and knowledge with others. To reach those lofty aspirations though, I first had to navigate through quite a few unexpected detours in my life. Though I was brought up in a religious family, it did not help me hear the messages from my spirit guide, Bodhi. If anything, religion only further isolated me, teaching me to accept the ego's view of religion rather than Bodhi's. It was not until after I stopped following a formal religion, I finally was able to embrace spirituality, and with this embrace, I awoke.

Spirituality is the belief there is a piece of god, a spirit, within everything that has life, and, because of this, all life is important, equal, and connected. After I awoke, no longer having the dogma of religion handicapping my views, I was suddenly free to explore this philosophy of life more deeply. Only then did I become aware of the mask I wore and the impenetrable wall I had erected around my heart; the mask and wall allowed me to survive in the world. I would always smile, appear happy, though I would often feel intense anxiety within. This was something I never really understood until the moment I confronted my ego. Little did I know these survival mechanisms would have a profound effect on me for the majority of my life. By protecting me from emotional pain, they also isolated me from my family, everyone else in my life, and even from myself. No one could hurt me because I did not allow anyone to get close enough to do so. In turn, no one could love me or was I able to truly love another either. This superficial life, one devoid of risk or pain, left me alone in a sea of people.

It took many years before the first cracks in my wall formed and before I could loosen the mask I constantly wore. It took me almost an entire lifetime to awaken and begin my journey toward enlightenment.

After I was clearly able to hear my spirit guide, Bodhi, I realized everything I had learned from my ego throughout my life was untrue. I had looked for love and happiness in the job I had, the money I made, things I owned, and through my wife and children. With the exception of the latter, I finally realized none of those things truly mattered. This does not mean I am ungrateful to my ego, however. It taught me coping skills and allowed me to succeed, or at least what I thought success was. Though my ego still remains with me, it has taken a more secondary role in my life now, relinquishing its former primary role to my spirit guide, Bodhi.

Decisions were now required. While it was tempting to take this newly found state of being, withdraw from society and all the hate, fear, cruelty, poverty, and greed that plagues it, I knew within myself, this knowledge was to be shared with others. That is my destiny. Therefore, I have written A Mystical Trilogy: *'Our Search for Meaning'*: a series of three books of thoughtful easily understandable spiritual reflections about life; A Spiritual Duology: *'Spiritual Reflections'*: two books of spiritual reflections using metaphor, imagery, and spiritual insight to explore themes of awakening, enlightenment, and the human pursuit of meaning; and *The Awakening Tetralogy* : the first three stories in *The Awakening Tetralogy* follow the spiritual journey through life of a child, as they learn the lessons needed during their life to awaken and become enlightened. It is my hope you will read these books, and in doing so, begin a new adventure; one where you will awaken and further your journey toward enlightenment with your spirit within.

I do not know if these books will be widely read in my lifetime, though I hope one day they may help others awaken and find enlightenment as well.

"We are all on a spiritual journey of love & peace;
together may we spread light throughout the world."

To read more of Ken's life-changing reflections visit his website:
kenluball.com[2]

Addendum

Glossary

<u>Asleep</u> – After we are born we are taught how to survive in the world and what success is. We therefore learn to worry only about our own success and survival in the world, rather than to be concerned about others. This results in living in a self-centered world of prejudice, inequity, and endless struggle. Those who fully believe this are asleep, accepting the status quo as the truth.

 <u>Awaken</u> – There may come a time in our life when, despite our success in the world, we begin to question the truth of our self-centered learned beliefs, our ego. When this happens the first quiet messages of the spirit, a piece of god present within every life are sensed, beginning us on an enduring journey to discover meaning in our life.

 <u>Ego</u> – The ego is everything we learn, believe, and accept is true after we are born, as we learn how to survive in a self-centered world. Its primary concern is what is best for us; it worries little about others. It also attempts to build up our self-esteem by convincing us of our value in the world.

 <u>Enlightenment</u> – The complete acceptance of the spiritual path, allowing the spirit's inherent wisdom and unconditional love to be our primary guide in life. With enlightenment, the ego, our self-centered learned beliefs, assumes a secondary role in our life, no longer influencing the direction of our life choices.

 <u>Spirit/ Soul/ God / Higher-Self</u> – An ethereal entity accompanying and inextricably connecting every life to another's. Its purpose is to give our lives meaning by sharing its inherent wisdom and unconditional love to help guide our life's choices.

 <u>Spirituality</u> – Spirituality is the belief there is a piece of god, a spirit or soul within every life intimately linking each of us to the other, and, because of this, each life, regardless of our differences, accomplishments, or genus, is important, equal, and connected.

What Happened to the Hippie Generation?
(Though this is written about the hippie generation,
it could just as easily be written about any generation)

When we were young, we
    were idealistic and going
to change the world.
We understood the meaning of
life was to share our love
selflessly with all others.
Sex, drugs, and rock & roll
was our mantra. Life was good.
As we got older though, our
lives became more challenging.
We had families, bills, and began
to forget why we were born.
Many of us began to accept
societies definition of success.
Rather than selflessly focusing
on what was best for everyone,
we began instead to concentrate
only on our accomplishments
and what was best for our
family and ourselves.
Instead of sharing our love
freely without conditions with
all others, as we once inherently
knew when we were young,
our job, amount of money
we made, material possessions
and other worldly things
soon defined our existence.
As our generation begins

to enter the twilight of our
lives it is not time to just
reminisce about our youth.
Instead, we must finish what
we began so many years ago
by spreading unconditional
love, peace, and light
around the world.
We must leave our children
a world in which they can
flourish; one where they can
share these idealistic spiritual
values not only with their
children, but with each other
and all life on our planet as well.
We must not live in
the past any longer.
It is time for all of us to rise
and change the direction of our
world, as we once hoped to do.
If we do not, our lives will have
been lived in vain, without
purpose or meaning, and we
will leave our children an
uninhabitable world of
fear, prejudice, and distrust.

We Are All Children of the World

Regardless of the color
    of our skin, ethnicity,
    religion, whether we are
    rich or poor, famous or
    unknown, or any other

comparison we may
make, we are all
children of the world.
No one life, regardless
of our differences or
accomplishments, is
or ever has been
better, more important,
than another's.
Apart, though some
may be more successful,
we will all fail.
Only together, by putting
our trivial differences
aside, may we all
flourish, and discover
genuine meaning in
our lives as well.

Reviewing My Life

I am in the twilight of life;
 death will come soon.
 I have no fear, though as I
 look back over my life, there
 are many things I wish
 I had done differently.
 Instead of worrying only
 about myself and success in
 the world, constantly working,
 striving to enjoy life, I would
 have spent more time helping
 others and with those I love.
 I would have listened, learned,
 and assisted all those in need,
 even strangers I did not know.
 I would have fought harder to
 change the world, feed the hungry,
 provide shelter to the homeless,
 and stop the prejudice, hate, and
 senseless slaughter humanity
 needlessly inflicts on each other.
 I only wish I had understood
 these things earlier, so my life
 could have been more meaningful,
 rather than simply being focused
 on only what was best for myself.

The Bird

Soaring in the sky, wings
    outstretched, gracefully
    riding the currents of wind,
    the bird majestically
    embraces is destiny.
    The higher the bird climbs,
    the more difficult its
    journey, due to the thin
    air and lack of oxygen.
    When it remains close to
    the ground, it feels secure
    in its environment.
    It is only when the bird
    challenges its confines though,
    soaring high above, will it
    truly see the world below,
    discovering the genuine
    beauty of life.
    Humanity is very
    much like the bird.
    When we remain in our
    comfort zone, fearing to soar
    and challenge our self-centered
    beliefs, we will never see
    life's true potential.
    It is only when we rise
    above, confront our fears,
    climb to new heights, may
    we begin a quest to
    understand our true
    life's purpose.

The Sun

As the sun rises, our
life begins anew.
With our birth, the sheer
beauty and clarity of all
it illuminates is apparent.
With our exposure to the world,
however, the suns brilliance
begins to fade, as its light
is partially hidden behind
the clouds above.
For some, only a few clouds
exist, allowing the sun's
rays to periodically reach
the ground below.
For others though, the clouds
darken, covering the entire sky.
How overcast the skies become
depends on our acceptance of
all we learned to be true.
Those who have fully
embraced this truth, though
they may find success in the
world, will perpetually live
under a darkened overcast
sky, one where the sun's
rays are seldom seen.
Only those who start to
challenge their self-centered
beliefs will begin to see
the clouds dissipate.
Though few will ever

observe the crystal clear
blue sky we once observed
with our birth, the journey
to see once again an
unblemished blue sky
is what makes life
truly worthwhile.

The Waterfall

In early spring, water melting
    from faraway mountain peaks,
    rush downward to the valley below.
    Before it reaches its destination,
    the water is calm, peaceful.
    It is only when it descends
    over an elevated bluff, its
    intensity increases, as it
    produces a beautiful,
    majestic waterfall.
    Humanity may be contrasted
    to a waterfall.
    Before we are born we are
    calm, peaceful, wise, knowing
    only unconditional love.
    It is not until we enter the
    world, socialized to accept
    the self-centered beliefs of
    society, our understanding
    about life's purpose
    becomes distorted.
    The true irony of life is
    we then spend the rest of
    our lives, trying to return
    to the calm, peaceful reflections
    and feelings of love we once
    knew before we were first born.

Givers and Takers

There are two types of
　　people: givers and takers.
　　A giver is someone who
　　shares their love freely
　　with all others, wanting
　　only the best for everyone.
　　A taker worries only about
　　themselves, unafraid to
　　take advantage of another.
　　Though a taker may be
　　successful in life, they
　　will never experience true
　　love, inner peace or learn
　　the lessons we are alive
　　to understand.
　　A giver, however, will
　　find these in abundance,
　　while also discovering life's
　　genuine intentions as well.

We Are Stronger Together

When you are down,
    struggling to hold
    on, I will be there.
    It matters not if
    we know each other.
    I will always offer my
    hand to hold you, my
    love to embrace you,
    and my soul to
    caress your wounds.
    We are stronger together.
    If you ever wondered
    why we are born,
    this is the reason.
    To selflessly help and
    love each other in
    our time of need.

You Are Worthwhile

Though you may be
    poor, struggle daily to
    survive, your life is as
    important as any other
    that has achieved success
    in the world.
    Our body is but a shell,
    housing our spirit within.

Our mind is but a tool
to accept society's beliefs.
Who we truly are, lies
not in our success or
thoughts, but in our
essence within.

The Ceiling

Above me the ceiling limits
    my view of the world,
    restricting my vision.
    I realize, above its confines,
    lies an extraordinary
    unrestricted realm,
    waiting to embrace me
    with its inherent wisdom
    and unconditional love.
    Like the ceiling, most of
    us limit our view of the
    world, only believing what
    we were taught, seeing our
    life limited by its boundaries.
    It is only when we observe
    what is above the ceiling,
    by challenging our self-
    centered beliefs, the
    beauty and genuine
    possibilities life offers
    may truly be discovered.

The Aurora

The picturesque colorful
    lights dance in the night
    sky, powered by solar
    wind speeding through
    the earth's atmosphere.
    Most are unable to see
    this spectacular display,
    as it is generally only
    seen at the extreme
    corners of our planet.
    Despite where we live
    though, we each may be
    able to see an aurora
    in our life as well.
    To do so, we must light
    up our darkened core,
    by traveling to the
    far corners within.
    We may do this by
    selflessly sharing the
    wisdom and unconditional
    love of our spirit within,
    then allowing it to guide
    all of our life's choices.

A Moment of Sanity

We live in a chaotic self-
    obsessed world, struggling

to survive the onslaught
of daily challenges.
To endure in such a world,
we must rely on ourselves
and what we need
to do to survive.
Every once in a while,
though, a passing thought
may penetrate our protective
exterior, our façade,
questioning our beliefs
and path through life.
This brief awakening creates
a moment of unbelievable
calm, inner peace, and
feelings of authentic love,
as a glimpse of what
discovering genuine
meaning in our life
reveals itself.

Only Together May We All Flourish

Every soul regardless of our
    differences, accomplishments,
    or genus, deserves to be
    helped in their time of need,
    and treated with unconditional
    love, selflessly shared
    without motive or benefit.
    There is never a reason to do otherwise.
    No one is, or ever has been
    better, their life more
    important, than another's.

We will never understand
our life's genuine purpose
unless we realize only together
may we all flourish.
Apart, regardless how
successful our life has been,
it will have been led
without meaning or purpose.

The Sky

On a clear day, we may
see far away mountains as
we gaze at the azure sky.
The purity of our view is
unobstructed; no impediments
obscure our vision.
Humanity may be
contrasted to the sky.
When we allow our acquired
self-centered beliefs and opinions
to cloud our lives, our vision
is obstructed as life's
challenges overwhelm us.
For some, their view is
so impeded, they are
nearly blind, unable
to see anything but
hate, fear, anger.
On those days though, when
we let down our shield, allowing
our spirit within to influence
our decisions, the sky once
again starts to brighten, as

we begin a quest to rediscover
the genuine path through life
we were always meant to follow.

Only Together May We Find Meaning

A small part of god exists
within every life, inextricably
connecting each to the other.
Apart we are weak, lost,
existing, though not truly
not living or experiencing
life as it was meant to be.
If we live our life like this,
though we may have been
successful and accomplished
much in our life, our life will
end without discovering
authentic love or the
genuine reason for
our life's journey.
Only together, selflessly
helping each other will
our lives be truly worthwhile
and the true meaning
of life be understood.

Every Life is Important

Humanity believes since
    they are the dominant species
    on our planet, their life is
    more important than other
    less evolved life forms.
    There are some who even
    believe, the lives of those
    who are different than them,
    as not as valuable as theirs.
    This self-centered view of
    the world is the cause of
    many of humanity's self-
    inflicted problems, harmful
    emotions, and actions,
    throughout their domination
    on our planet.
    In reality, every life,
    regardless of genus,
    appearance, or
    accomplishments, is
    equally important.
    Only when humanity
    starts to understand this,
    may their spiritual
    evolution truly begin.

When We See Another

When we see another, do

we look at their physical
body or the presence within each?
Our form is but a shell,
sheltering a spirit, a piece
of god within, present to
help guide our life with
its innate wisdom and
unconditional love, to
provide meaning and
purpose in our lives.
Those who only see our
physical self, believing its
appearance defines us,
though their life may be
successful and their body
pleasant to view, will lead
a life without purpose or meaning.
Only those who peer deeply
into the eyes, the soul of
another, seeing beyond
their superficial physique
and façade they present
to the world, will truly
discover another's
genuine worth.

The Guru

One does not need a guru,
    a spiritual teacher, to
    understand spirituality.
    Though the sage may have

traveled further on the path
toward enlightenment,
within each person, the
identical wisdom is, and
has always existed.
Humanity's greatest spiritual
leaders, Jesus, Mohammed,
and Buddha, understood this.
We each may join these
gurus in their desire to
selflessly help others,
by embracing our own
spiritual core, present
within each, allowing
it to be the primary
guide in our life.

As Death Approaches

Many go through life asleep,
    believing everything they
    were taught is true.
    Though they may become
    wealthy, famous, have a
    prestigious job, they will
    never experience true
    love or know the genuine
    reason they were granted life.
    As death approaches, when
    they review their life, they
    may finally understand their
    wealth, fame, job, were not
    very important and did
    not define who they truly are.
    It is then they may finally
    understand, we are spirit,
    alive to selflessly share our
    spirit's innate wisdom and
    unconditional love to help
    all others understand who
    they truly are as well.

Treat Others With Kindness

Any slight to another,
    regardless of form,
    harms both.
    Every interaction not
    predicated on kindness,
    weakens our world and
    our ability to discover
    life's genuine purpose.
    Always treat everyone,
    regardless of differences,
    with unconditional love.
    Doing so, will not only
    help further the spiritual
    evolution of our planet,
    but also allow each of
    us to experience true
    happiness, inner peace,
    and discover the genuine
    meaning of life as well.

Undoing the Damage

When we are first born,
the damage begins.
As we learn what is
expected of us, we
start to accept the
self-centered beliefs
of the world around us.
For most, these beliefs
impede the underlying
messages of their spirit,
a piece of god, present
within each of us.
Though the ego will
always remain, helping
us survive in the world,
only by allowing the spirit,
rather than the ego, to be
the primary guide in our
life, will the damage
which began were young,
be mitigated, and the
genuine purpose of our
life's journey be understood.

Taking Advantage of Others

There is never a reason
to do, say, or imply

harm to another.
It matters not if the
slight is verbal, physical,
or in any other manner.
We are all in life's
journey together.
Though many believe the
injury they caused to the
other is trivial, in reality,
it harms both.
Apart, regardless of our
success or accomplishments
in life, our lives
are insignificant.
Only together, by always
helping others and treating
all with respect and
unconditional love, will
life's genuine meaning
become apparent.

Living in a Split Reality

We live in a world where
  two truths exist simultaneously.
  One we can see, as we view
  the constant struggles and
  hardships of so many
  around the world.
  Those existing in this self-
  centered reality, believe their
  indoctrination into society,
  accepting the loneliness and
  numerous challenges
  accompanying these
  beliefs result in.
  The other truth resides
  within each of us, recognizing
  unconditional love as its mantra.
  This reality realizes only by
  selflessly helping each other
  will we all survive and
  find purpose in our life.
  Most exist living on a
  continuum between these
  two realities.
  Only those though, who
  embrace the latter, will
  discover true happiness,
  boundless love, inner peace,
  and understand the genuine
  meaning of life as well.

What is Normal?

It is not normal to live
    in a world of greed,
    prejudice, inequity; of
    hunger, war, homelessness.
    Accepting living in such
    a world is considered
    normal by many;
    it is not.
    The normal world we are
    supposed to live in is a
    world of love, compassion,
    and equality, one where
    we help each other
    in times of need.
    Only when humanity
    redefines its definition
    of normal and truly
    understands this, may
    the spiritual evolution
    of our planet finally begin.

We're So Vain

Humanity believes their
lives are more important
than all other forms of
life, and the planet that
enables their survival.
They even believe, the
lives of some, due to their
race, ethnicity, wealth, or
any number of other
differences, are more
valuable than others.
This arrogant view of the
world is the cause of many
of humanity's problems.
War, hunger, prejudice,
inequity, are just a few of
the numerous challenges
resulting from the belief
in their superiority.
After we awaken, sensing
the first messages from our
spirit within, we begin to
question these beliefs.
With the realization every
life, each with a spirit, a
piece of god within, is equally
important and must be
respected and helped in
their time of need, we
begin in earnest our
journey to discover the

genuine meaning of life.

See Beyond Our Differences

Though we are all
different in many
ways, it is our similarities
that must unite us.
Look beyond appearance,
beliefs, accomplishments,
to see the genuine soul,
the essence of another.
If you do, you will find
we are truly one, united
by a universal spirit,
intimately connecting
us to each other.
Despite our many
differences, we each
have a small piece
of god within.
Recognizing this common
bond, unites us all
together as one.

Love Unites Us

Though we all look and
　　believe differently, it is love
　　that unites us as one.
　　Intimately linked together
　　by a unifying spirit present
　　within each, our life's quest
　　is to selflessly share our
　　unconditional love with
　　all others, helping each
　　in their time of need.
　　To discover life's genuine
　　purpose, open your heart,
　　and release your infinite love
　　within, for the benefit all.

Judging Others

In the self-centered world
    we live in, many judge and
    demean others due to their
    race, ethnicity, beliefs,
    or any number of
    other differences we
    use to justify our
    superiority to another.
    They, therefore, often
    ignore and treat those
    they feel inferior with
    indifference.
    When we awaken,
    sensing the first messages
    from our spirit within,
    we realize no one life,
    regardless of
    accomplishments,
    appearance, or any
    other possible comparison,
    each with a spirit, a piece
    of god within, is or every
    has been, more important
    than another's.

Why is There?

Why is there hate,
    prejudice, hunger, and
    numerous other struggles
    experienced by so many?
    Why is there a sense of
    entitlement, feeling some
    are superior, their life
    more important than
    another's, due to
    their differences or
    accomplishments
    in life?
    Though we look, act,
    believe differently, we
    are all one, intimately
    linked by a universal
    spirit, a piece of god
    present within each.
    No one life is or ever
    has been better
    than another's.
    Only when humanity
    truly understands this,
    may the needless struggles
    be mitigated, and our
    planet's spiritual evolution
    finally begin.

Helping Each Other

We are alive to help,
    not harm each other.
    Yet, due to our self-
    centered upbringing,
    we have forgotten
    the reason for our
    life's journey.
    We awaken when
    we begin to hear
    the first messages
    from our spirit within
    reminding us of our
    true purpose in life.
    We become enlightened
    when we fully embrace
    its inherent wisdom and
    unconditional loving
    beliefs, then selflessly
    share those to help
    all in need.

A World of Kindness, Empathy, and Love

How can we accept the
  senseless demise of another;
  the hunger, lack of shelter,
  or any other needless struggles
  suffered by anyone?
  All these hardships
  need not exist.
  They are caused by living
  in a self-centered world of
  greed, prejudice, and entitlement.
  Our planet is careening
  toward an abyss, one we
  may not be able to prevent
  our descent into.
  We may only reverse
  this inevitable outcome,
  by sincerely helping and
  loving each other,
  assuring every person,
  regardless of our
  differences, may survive,
  and be able to thrive in
  a world of kindness,
  empathy, and love.

Finding Love and Happiness

We search the world to
     find love and happiness.
     Though we may believe
     we have found them,
     often they are temporary,
     fleeting, like a passing
     storms rain.
     These things may not
     be found in a self-
     centered world.
     To find genuine love
     and happiness, look within,
     then selflessly share your
     love and happiness to
     help others find them
     in their life as well.

Every Life is Equally Valuable

There are some who
believe, due to their
race, religion, wealth,
job, or any of hundreds
of other differences,
their life is more
important than another's.
This is true not only of
humanity, but also their
beliefs about all other
forms of life as well.
Peer deeply into
the eyes of another
sentient life form.
If you do, you will see
their spirit, the same
piece of god present
within us, intimately
linking us all together.
Every life, therefore,
regardless of their
accomplishments,
appearance, or
form, each with a
piece of god within,
is, and has always
been, equally valuable.

Open Your Eyes

How long may we close
    our eyes, pretending
    we do not see?
    How many more years
    may we continue to
    ignore the pain, tears,
    senseless deaths, and
    struggles of others,
    while we do nothing?
    We must all open our
    eyes, pretend no more,
    selflessly helping all
    in need, allowing each
    to live their life with
    dignity, hope, and
    eternal love.

Our Children are Watching

Our children see, hear,
    and adopt the beliefs of
    the self-centered world
    they are to live in.
    They, therefore, learn about
    hate, prejudice, greed, and
    the value of worrying only
    about themselves, while
    ignoring the many
    struggles of others.
    Most of humanity's problems,
    conflicts, and harmful emotions,
    are the result of living
    in such a world.
    It need not be this way;

there is another path
we may follow:
the spiritual path.
It is one of unconditional
love, selflessly helping each
other, aiding all in
their time of need.
This path rejects the
learned egoistic views
of the world, believing
instead we are alive to
sincerely care about
each other.
Our children are watching.
Let us raise them to accept
the latter path through life,
allowing humanity to
evolve and our children
to flourish in a world
of hope, peace, and
unconditional love.

I Was Blind, But Now I See

Living in a self-centered
     world, most believe what
     they learn as they are
     socialized to accept the
     mores of society.
     This narrow vision of life
     blinds them to the genuine
     possibilities life offers,
     and is the cause of many
     of humanity's self-inflicted
     challenges, harmful emotions,
     and needless struggles.
     Only by removing our blinders,
     questioning our learned beliefs,
     will we begin to finally see
     and understand our true
     purpose in life: to selflessly
     share, love, and help each
     other, regardless of our
     differences, through
     life's many challenges.

Blaming Others

Many spend their entire
    life blaming other people
    and life situations for their
    struggles and unhappiness,
    never accepting responsibility
    for their own failings.
    We are all exposed to many
    challenges in our lives.
    It is how we respond
    to them that will
    determine our burden.
    Those who have accepted
    society's self-centered beliefs,
    seldom accept blame for
    their actions or struggles.
    Only those who never fault
    another, understanding
    their experiences in life
    are part of the journey,
    will begin on a quest to
    discover the genuine
    meaning of life.

Labels

Humanity uses labels to
differentiate everyone.
Male, female, rich, poor,
black, white, Christian,
Muslim, are but a few
of the numerous ways
we distinguish ourselves
from each other.
Though some labels are
necessary to prevent
confusion, they also divide,
rather than unite us.
Prejudice, hate, feelings of
superiority, are but three of
many emotions resulting
from our inconsequential
differences.
In reality, there is but
one label that may be
used to truly describe
humanity and all life.
We are spirit, a piece of
god present within every
life, alive to selflessly share
our inherent wisdom and
unconditional love with
all others, regardless
of our differences or
accomplishments in life.
Anything else is an illusion,
created by the ego, our

learned beliefs, to challenge
our choices in life.

Living in a World of Love

View the world with love.
    See only the best in others;
    ignore the façade they
    have created to help them
    survive in a self-centered world.
    If we do this, there will no
    longer be greed, prejudice,
    inequity; no harmful
    emotions or unnecessary
    struggles resulting from
    living in an egoistic world.
    All excess will be shared,
    all judgments suspended,
    all conflicts ended.
    All that will be left is
    unconditional love,
    shared selflessly with
    others, for the benefit of all.

How Many More?

How many more innocents
    must die before we finally
    recognize their loss?
    How many more children
    must needlessly perish from
    war, starvation, random violence?
    How much longer will we
    tolerate prejudice, hate,
    inequity, the endless suffering
    of others, before we finally see
    and do something to help
    those who are struggling?
    We each must answer these
    questions ourselves: to
    continue to accept the self-
    centered status quo, or to
    sincerely recognize these
    harmful beliefs and actions
    resulting in the challenges
    of so many.
    Only when we acknowledge
    the truth of what is happening,
    and actively attempt to correct
    these injustices, may lasting
    change help end these
    travesties and our world
    truly begin its spiritual evolution.

Freedom

We each have the freedom
　　to make choices in our life.
　　We may choose to embrace
　　our individual needs and
　　desires, even if these may
　　cause pain or struggle to others.
　　Or we may decide to help
　　those in need, selflessly
　　sharing our excess and love,
　　mitigating the many challenges
　　humanity has inflicted on itself.
　　We know the results of
　　pursuing the former path.
　　Perhaps it is time to sincerely
　　consider others in all our
　　words, actions, and deeds,
　　ensuring a future for all,
　　rather than continue to
　　be concerned only for
　　our own freedom.

Caring About Each Other

Every action we take
    must not harm another.
    Every word we say must
    be spoken with love, not malice.
    Every person we meet must
    be treated with respect and
    kindness, not contempt
    and animosity.
    There is never a reason
    to do otherwise.
    We are each meant to
    sincerely care and help
    each other through life's
    many trials, not to hate
    and hinder another to
    benefit only ourselves.

Life's Genuine Purpose

How many people must
    needlessly die before
    we say no more?
    How many others must
    suffer, while we ignore
    their pleas for help?
    How many innocent children,
    too young to understand why,
    must go hungry, be homeless,
    before we open our eyes and see?
    Is one life more important
    than another's?
    If you believe it is, then
    though you may be successful
    and live to an old age, your
    life will have been lived
    without meaning or purpose.
    If, however, you realize
    every life, regardless of our
    differences or accomplishments,
    is equally valuable, and
    selflessly share your inherent
    wisdom and unconditional
    love, your spirit, with each,
    then you will have discovered
    life's genuine purpose.

What is Our Value?

Many determine the value
    of another by their wealth,
    fame, job; the color of their
    skin, ethnicity, religion.
    Those who believe the
    worth of another may be
    judged by these superficial
    traits, though they may be
    successful, have completely
    misunderstood the true
    meaning of life.
    There may time a time in
    our life though when we
    begin to question if what
    we were taught and thought
    to be true, really was the truth.
    Only when we genuinely
    understand little of it was,
    may we begin to know
    the true worth of another
    may not be found in a
    self-centered world.
    Rather it may only be
    discovered within each of
    us, then is must be selflessly
    shared to help others
    understand this as well.

Is One Life More Important Than Another?

Some believe the lives of

those who are wealthy,
intelligent, have a prestigious
job, or are a certain race,
ethnicity, religion, are more
important than those who
are poor, unknown, a minority,
or working a menial job.
Absolutely none, not one of
these differences, or any
other comparisons we may
make, makes one life more
important than another's.
Every single life, regardless
of success, appearance, or
beliefs, is and has always
been, equally valuable,
each deserving to be helped
when in need, and treated
as we ourselves wish
others to treat us.

Be a Good Person

Though the world we live
    in does not concern itself
    with pleasantries,
    emphasizing only the
    needs of ourselves, rather
    than others, there is never
    a reason not to be kind,
    considerate, to another.
    Words and deeds may
    severely harm someone.
    Everything we say and action
    we take should therefore be
    shared with love, always
    emphasizing the good,
    rather than only
    seeking out the bad.

A World of Hope

To change the world, we
each must selflessly share
our spirit, a piece of god
present within every life,
to spread its innate wisdom
and unconditional love
with all others.
It matters not our differences,
appearance, accomplishments,
or any other possible comparison
we may choose to make.
It also should not consider if
the other is someone we know
or a stranger we have never met.
Our spirit gives our lives purpose.
It accompanies each of us
through our life's journey,
inextricably linking us
to each other.
Only by sincerely helping,
caring, and loving each other,
will humanity evolve, allowing
our children to grow up in a
world of hope, rather than
continue to live in a
world of despair.

A Sensitive Heart

Living in a harsh, often
    cruel self-centered world,
    it is difficult to genuinely
    care about another, fearful of
    them one day causing us harm.
    It matters not if the injury is
    verbal, physical, emotional,
    or any other form of suffering.
    By trusting someone, we
    expose our vulnerabilities,
    our heart, to another.
    We therefore protect ourselves
    by hardening our heart, not
    allowing anyone to hurt us.
    Though this prevents us
    from experiencing severe
    pain and disappointment,
    it also inhibits our genuine
    feelings and emotions, hidden
    within, from being shared.
    To truly experience love
    though, we must risk pain,
    opening our vulnerable heart
    to another, to allow our pure
    genuine affections and
    unconditional love
    to be revealed.

Let It Go

Being angry, upset at
    another, harms both,
    separating us from each other.
    By holding onto the injury,

it inhibits our divine growth.
The insult, and our reaction
to it, results from our self-
centered vulnerabilities
we both learned when we
were young to protect us
from harmful words or
actions by another.
To be able to awaken,
and begin our spiritual
journey, we must let go
of these negative feelings,
whole-heartedly forgiving
the other for their human
failings, and embrace them,
as we do all others, with
unconditional love.

The Glass

The water in the crystal
    clear glass is half gone.
    Most see the glass partially
    empty, believing before
    the water nears the bottom,
    they must do all the things
    they were told would allow
    them to be successful
    and enjoy their life.
    They work hard, get an
    education, make money,
    buy material possessions,
    allowing them to be happy
    before their glass empties.
    The rest see the glass half
    full, realizing there is much
    more to learn then just
    what we were taught.
    They strive to refill their
    glass of water to the top
    by helping others realize
    that most of the self-
    centered views we were
    brought up to believe are
    true, never have been.
    As their glass of water
    approaches the top once
    more, they understand the
    genuine purpose of life is
    to unconditionally love
    each other, selflessly aiding

all, regardless of our differences,
so we each may fill our glass
to the top and experience a
life blessed with love, peace,
happiness, and meaning.

Our Angry Planet

Stop.
   Listen.
   Our world is in pain.
   The earth, once pure and
   untouched, now cries in
   agony as it is being destroyed
   by humanity's avarice.
   Its rage is reflected by
   worsening disasters, as the
   human race thoughtlessly
   pollutes its land, water, and air.
   If change is not imminent,
   our planet will simply wait
   until our species, like so
   many others, becomes extinct,
   then, over time, without
   humanity's uncaring presence,
   it will restore its grandeur,
   returning, once again, to the
   pristine world it once was.

The Lighthouse

The lighthouse overlooks
    the beautiful blue ocean,
    its waves roaring over jagged
    rocks near the sandy shore.
    In the distance, the sound of
    isolated vessels blare their
    horns, imploring the
    lighthouse to shine its bright
    light toward them, so they may
    avoid hitting the nearby barriers.
    As with the lighthouse, we each
    have a light within us as well,
    present to help us avoid the
    many difficult choices that
    may cause us harm every day.
    To discover this light, stop,
    listen silently to the quiet voice
    in between your chaotic thoughts,
    then follow the wisdom and
    unconditional loving advice
    it so desperately tries
    to get you to listen to.

Our Divisions

Humanity endlessly divides
    everyone into castes,
    artificially isolating us
    from each other.
    Race, religion, wealth,
    ethnicity, are but four
    of the innumerable ways
    we differentiate ourselves
    from others.
    For those who are poor,
    a minority, living in a
    distant land, their destiny
    is often predetermined from
    the moment of their birth.
    These differences serve
    only to isolate us from each
    other, rather than unite us.
    In truth, though we may
    appear, act, or believe
    differently than another,
    within, we are all the same.
    We are spirit, alive to
    understand, accept, and
    embrace our spiritual core,
    then selflessly share its
    innate wisdom and
    unconditional loving
    messages to help all in need.

The Victim

We are only victims if
　　we allow ourselves to be.
　　Though others may, at times,
　　take advantage of us, it is
　　how we react that will
　　determine the slight.
　　Everyone, without exception,
　　has flaws, resulting from
　　accepting the self-centered
　　beliefs we were taught
　　when we were young.
　　The harm another causes us,
　　resulting from their upbringing,
　　does not represent who
　　they truly are.
　　See beyond the abuse and
　　the illusional façade, to the
　　genuine soul within another,
　　to realize they would never
　　judge or harm another.
　　Doing so, will permit us to
　　discard the pain, never allowing
　　us to be a victim again.

The Complainer

There are some who complain
about everything, never
learning from the lessons
they are presented.
Instead, they blame others,
bad luck, the world itself,
for their misfortunes,
struggles, and unhappiness.
Those who spend their lives
like this, though they may
find a little satisfaction if
their complaint is successful,
will never understand the
reason they were presented
these challenges, nor learn
from these opportunities.
It is only those who never
complain, embracing every
challenge life presents with
vigor, who will face the
affront and learn from
the lesson being offered.

Judging Others

Many judge others determining
    their worth by their distinctions.
    Judgment only divides us,
    resulting in many of humanity's
    challenges and harmful emotions.
    Though we are all different
    in many ways, we have
    no right to judge another.
    Each, though unique, has
    a spirit, a piece of god
    accompanying them
    through their life's journey.
    No one person, therefore,
    each with a piece of god
    within, is, or ever has been
    better, their life more
    important than another's.
    Only when humanity stops
    judging others, may the
    spiritual evolution of our
    planet finally begin.

Who Are We?

Many believe who they are
    is determined by their
    circumstances in life.
    Race, ethnicity, wealth, are
    but a few of the hundreds of

ways we identify ourselves
in a divided world, separating,
rather than uniting us
with each other.
In truth, though we may appear,
act, and believe differently,
we are spirit, each having a
piece of god within, intimately
linking us to each other.
Our life's purpose is to put
aside our petty differences,
embrace our similarities by
accepting the wisdom and
unconditional loving guidance
of our spirit, then selflessly
sharing its messages of peace,
love, and light, with all
others, so they too may
understand and share these
messages as well.

We Are All Family

Though we may not know
someone, look or believe
differently than they do,
we are all related, connected
by a common bond,
inextricably linking
us together.
We are each part of the
extended family of humanity,
alive to help each other,
regardless of our differences,

by selflessly sharing our
inherent wisdom and
unconditional love, our
spirit, for the benefit of all.

The Right to Exist

Since humanity has dominion
over all living things on our
planet, they feel entitled to
take advantage of their weaknesses.
They therefore exploit, abuse,
and senselessly kill other life
forms, unconcerned about
their right to exist.
There are even some who
think, because of their
outward differences and
beliefs, they are more
entitled than others of
their own species as well.
Every life has a spirit, a
piece of god accompanying
it, there to give its life
purpose and meaning,
connecting each life
to the other.
It matters not its genus,
appearance, or vulnerability.
Only when humanity truly
understands this, respecting
every life's right to exist, will
its spiritual evolution truly begin.

Intolerance

Intolerance is learned;
    it is not inherent.
    By judging another, we
    become prejudiced, needing
    to show our superiority to
    others due to our differences.
    Appearance, beliefs, wealth, are
    but three of the numerous ways
    we assess each other, needing
    to prove our preeminence.
    In truth, absolutely no one,
    regardless of our differences
    or accomplishments in life,
    is better, their life more
    important, than another's.
    Believing we are is the
    cause of many of humanity's
    problems and harmful beliefs.
    We are one, united by a
    universal spirit, equal
    in every way.
    Anything else, first thought
    to be true when we were young
    as we were indoctrinated
    into the world, is an illusion,
    meant to challenge
    our choices in life.

Honor Everyone

Living in a self-centered
world, concerned only for
what is best for ourself,
we tend to share ourselves
with another only if
it benefits us.
Though we may become
successful in such a world,
if our success was not
selflessly shared with
others, we will never
experience true happiness,
love, or discover
meaning in our life.
Only by truly respecting,
sharing, and honoring all
others, without focus on
ourself, will these precious
emotions be realized, allowing
us to discover our life's
genuine purpose as well.

The Eclipse

The blinding sun's rays,
emerging from its luminous
core, spread throughout the
solar system, providing light,
warmth, and nourishment,
to every life in its reach.
When the moon passes directly
in front of it, blocking its light,
we wait in darkness for its return.
As with the sun, we each

have a bright light within.
When its light is unencumbered,
we feel peaceful, happy, content.
However, when our light begins
to be inhibited, eclipsed by darkness
arising from stress, struggle, or
other challenges, our dimmed
light may instead result in
depression, despair, and uncertainty.
As with the passing of the
moon ending the eclipse,
our light may too shine
brightly once more as well.
To speed its passing, listen to the
quiet messages within, in between
your racing thoughts, then follow
                the loving messages you hear.

Another Choice

Humanity chooses to live
in a world of inequity,
prejudice, injustice.
Their choice is predicated
on accepting the self-
centered beliefs they were
brought up to believe were
normal; they are not.
These tenets are the underlying
cause of many of humanity's
problems and challenges in life.
There is another choice though;
one that will challenge all of
our fundamental convictions.

We may instead treat all others
with kindness, compassion,
and love, selflessly sharing
our excess and inherent
goodness with all in need.
This will not only bring
meaning to our lives,
but also further the
spiritual evolution of
our planet as well.

Dying of the Light

We are born with a
　　blinding light shining
　　so brightly darkness
　　cannot penetrate it.
　　From our first breath though,
　　our light begins to dim,
　　as we are taught to accept
　　the self-centered beliefs
　　of the world.
　　The more we believe what
　　we are taught, the dimmer
　　our light becomes.
　　As our light further loses its
　　luster, some may become
　　stressed, depressed, anxious,
　　struggling to find happiness,
　　inner peace, and love, in a
　　world these may never
　　be found in.
　　To rediscover our light,
　　it is necessary to abandon

the false self-centered beliefs
we once blindly accepted as
true, embracing, instead, the
inherent wisdom of unconditional
loving beliefs of the
spirit, our light, within.

Inequality

How do we justify inequality?
Depending on where you
were born, your upbringing,
the color of your skin, your
ability to get a good education,
or any number of other
differences, many struggle
daily to survive, while others
have the best life offers.
Accepting this paradigm
is the cause of greed,
prejudice, inequity.
It is also the underlying
cause of homelessness,
war, hunger, and numerous
other challenges experienced
by so many in the world.
Only when all our resources
are equally shared and our
belief in entitlement challenged,
may these problems finally
be addressed, and the spiritual
evolution of humanity truly begin.

The Fog of Life

It is drizzling, rain passing
through a thick fog,
disguising everything
surrounding it.
Beneath the fog, we walk
carefully, trying not to get wet.
We hide under an umbrella,
perhaps a doorway, waiting
for the rain to end.
Many of us go through life
in a fog, trying to avoid the
hurdles placed in front of us.
We struggle to avoid the rain
and fog, hiding from life,
accepting the illusions
we learned are true.
It is only by walking through
the rain and dense fog though,
not hiding in the doorways
and accepting everything we
thought was true, life may
finally be understood.
Once the fog of life evaporates,
all that is left is the spirit, a
piece of god present to give
our lives meaning by sharing
its inherent wisdom and
unconditional love to help
guide our life's choices.
Only then may a true
understanding about life

emerge, as the many false
illusions we learned as
children are finally recognized.

Our Aura

Others may observe much
   about us by the aura
  we radiate to the world.
  For many, stress, or any
  number of other daily
  challenges in life, darken
  the subtle non-verbal
  messages we each emit.
  The more we believe what
  we learned about how to
  survive and succeed in a
  self-centered world, the
  darker our aura becomes.
  To lighten our aura, lessen
  our stresses, and begin a
  journey to discover our
  true purpose in life, sit quietly,
  listen intently to the silence
  in between your racing
  thoughts, then embrace the
  wisdom and tender loving
  messages you hear within.

The Balcony

Looking down from the
    balcony we see a world
    in disarray; one where
    distrust, fear, and endless
    struggle manifest.
    Hate, prejudice, make some
    believe they are more
    deserving than others;
    they are not.
    Living in a self-centered
    world, focusing only on
    what is best for ourself,
    is the cause of these beliefs
    and many of humanity's
    challenges in life.
    Only when we accept
    everyone, regardless of
    our differences, is equal,
    important, and deserving,
    will our view from above
    change, seeing instead a
    world of equity, compassion,
    and universal love.

Priorities

The resources of our
    planet are exploited by
    the wealthy, for the
    benefit of the few.
    Humanity spends incredible
    amounts of money preparing
    or fighting wars, rather than

spending this money to
help those most in need.
They buy bombs and
bullets to kill people,
rather than food for the
hungry or to provide
shelter for the homeless.
This is insanity, solved only
by a paradigm shift; one that
requires putting the needs
of all before those of
the privileged few.

Happiness

Wishing to be happy,
      some buy nice things,
      have a family, try
      to enjoy life.
      This type of happiness
      though, is fleeting, lasting
      only until changes in our
      life circumstances
      end our bliss.
      To find true everlasting
      happiness, we must first
      reunite with our spirit within,
      then selflessly share its
      wisdom and unconditional
      love with all others.
      Only when we help others
      discover their happiness
      as well, may we truly

discover what happiness is.

.

Darkness and Light

Darkness results from
    embracing certain beliefs
    we learn when we are young.
    These beliefs then dominate
    our lives, as we react to
    the world around us.
    We learn to be self-centered,
    untrusting, fearful of
    being hurt by others.
    We may become indifferent
    to the prejudice, inequity,
    and struggles of others,
    as we try to survive in a
    harsh, often cruel world.
    Our guardrails not only
    shield us from harm,
    but also isolate us from
    others as well, hiding our
    light from the world.
    Light radiates from
    embracing our spirit,
    a piece of god present
    within every life, there to
    share its wisdom and
    unconditional love to help
    guide our life choices.
    We each have a choice
    which to follow:

darkness or light.
To discover life's true
purpose, choose the path
of light, then selflessly
share your light
with the world.

Our Journey Through Life

With our birth, from our
first breath, we learn how
to act, what to believe,
how to survive in a
self-centered world.
Though some of what we
learn is necessary, many
go through their entire
life never questioning
if these beliefs are true.
As we get older, some
may begin to wonder if
they really are true.
There is an uncertainty,
unrest within, telling
them it may not be.
With time, as we start to
confront the many untruths
we learned when we were
young, understanding few
of them were true, we begin
to realize we spent our entire
lives pursuing an illusion.
With the complete embrace

of the spiritual path, we find
the answers we have sought.
Selflessly sharing our
spirit's wisdom and
unconditional love with
others, we will also
discover our true purpose
in life as well.

How Long?

So much hate, fear,
    prejudice; so many
    needless deaths,
    hungry, homeless.
    How long will we
    allow this to continue?
    We are taught we cannot
    change the struggles
    so many endure.
    This is a lie, fabricated
    by a self-centered society
    to convince us to
    accept the status quo.
    We must each challenge
    this myth, embracing
    courage instead of fear,
    acceptance instead of
    prejudice, and love
    instead of hate.

The Eyes of a Child

When a young child sees
   the world, their view is
   not yet skewed by the
   dictates and traditions
   of the world.
   They see a world of
   endless possibilities,
   one where there is hope,
   love, and compassion.
   They have not yet learned
   to be cynical, prejudiced, uncaring.
   As they begin to get older
   though, they become fearful,
   as they are taught to accept
   the mores of society.
   Their innocence, once pure,
   has begun to fade, causing
   them to forget the path
   through life they were
   meant to pursue.
   Instead, they follow the
   self-centered illusional path
   they were told would bring
   them success and happiness.
   To change the direction of
   the world, save our planet
   from humanity's destructive
   tendencies, we all need to
   remember and embrace the
   world as it could be, when
   we first looked at it through

the eyes of a young child.

A Glimmer of Light

When we are born,
   our light illuminates
   the entire world.
   From that first moment
   though, its brightness
   begins to dull as we are
   taught how to survive in a
   self-centered harsh world.
   Despite our upbringing and
   challenges in life though,
   within every life lingers
   a glimmer of light.
   For some who have
   accepted most of the
   messages they learned,
   this light is quite dusky.
   For others it glows more
   brightly, as the original
   memory of our spirit within,
   still has some influence
   on their daily choices.
   It is not too late to change
   the direction of our life.
   By embracing and accepting the
   wisdom and unconditional loving
   messages of our spirit, once
   unimpeded by our learned
   illusions of life, our light
   may once again reemerge

and shine brightly, as it
was always meant to do.

Follow Your Heart

When we make decisions
in life, do we follow our
loving heart, or are our
decisions based on
what we learned?
Though there are occasions
these are the same, many
times the choices we make
would be quite different
depending on which
we are listening to.
The ego, our self-centered
beliefs, only considers
what is best for itself.
The spirit, however, not
only considers this, but
also is concerned for
what is best for everyone
else as well.
To find inner peace,
happiness, love, and
genuine meaning in
life, always follow
your heart.

The Darkness Behind Our Smile

To the entire world,
    we appear blessed.
    We have a good job,
    family, home.
    Our constant smile
    convinces the world of our
    happiness and accomplishments.
    Yet behind the smile, the facade
    we learned long ago to present
    to the world, lies a broken,
    unhappy, stressed, person.
    We became so good protecting
    ourself from those who would
    abuse us, we developed an
    alter ego, one that masked
    our internal struggle, allowing
    us to survive in a harsh,
    judgmental world.
    Though we project an image
    of a happy successful
    person, nothing could
    be further from the truth.
    Some of us have developed
    coping mechanisms, using
    drugs or drinking alcohol to
    bury their true emotions and feelings.
    To confront our darkness,
    we must first look within.
    Only by embracing and
    sharing the inherent wisdom
    and unconditional love of our
    spirit, realizing our genuine
    worth and importance does
    not lie in the self-centered
    world, but by selflessly

sharing our spirit's wisdom
and love with others, may
our darkness lighten,
beginning us on a journey
to discover the genuine
meaning of life.

We Are All Children of the World

We live is a very divided
world, separated by religion,
country, sex, wealth, race,
and other ways too numerous
to mention, justifying our
harmful beliefs and
actions toward others.
These differences are used
to rationalize war, hate,
prejudice, inequity.
Our dysfunctional world is
slowly falling into an abyss,
descending toward
its bottomless crater.
We must realize we are
all children of the world,
related by a common purpose
and spark of the divine
present within each.
Only by embracing love,
compassion, and equality,
helping all in need without
alternative intentions, may
the direction and future
of our world evolve,

allowing our planet and
all life on it to thrive.

Every Life is Sentient

Regardless if life is
    human, animal, or any
    other form of life existing
    in the vast universe, every
    life, each with a spark of
    the divine present within,
    is equally valuable.
    Though mankind is the
    dominant species on our
    planet, it does not mean
    our life is more significant
    than another's or
    another form of life.
    Everything alive has a right
    to exist, its life to be respected,
    and given an opportunity to
    discover its genuine purpose in life.

Judging Each Other

When we see another,
    we often decide what
    we think of them.
    We see their race, appearance,
    sex, and many other things
    we learned differentiate
    us from each other.

Even before they speak,
we often have formed
an opinion about them.
Though we do not
understand the challenges
they have had in their life,
or their beauty and love
existing within, we have
already decided if we
wish to spend time
getting to know them.
Every person, every life,
each with a spirit, a
piece of god within,
is a gift to all.
We are blessed to be
given the opportunity
to share in everyone's
passage through life.
Regardless of our
differences, we must
embrace each other,
without reservation
or judgment, selflessly
sharing our wisdom, love,
and essence, with every person.
Only then will life's true
purpose become evident.

Compassion, Love, and Humanity

We have always lived in
a very troubled world;

one where self-preservation
directs our beliefs,
thoughts, and actions.
We have therefore neglected
the needs of others, struggling
to survive in an indifferent world.
When we were young, before
we were exposed to the dictates
of the world, we once possessed
compassion and love.
With our socialization and
concern for only ourselves
and success in life though,
we lost our humanity.
To rediscover it, we must try
to remember what we once knew:
to selflessly share our compassion,
love, and humanity with all others,
without reservation, to help others
rediscover their compassion,
love and humanity as well.
Only then may our humanity
be restored, allowing each of
us to discover our true
purpose in life as well.
life's true purpose.

Our Children May Change the World

The first five years of
every child's life is
the most important.
It is during this time they
learn what is expected

of them and how they
will react to different
situations in the world.
It is also when they will
develop an overall view of
humanity and how to treat others.
Their opinions, prejudices,
beliefs, and aspirations, often
begin during these early
formative years, and will
form the basis of how they
will act and think about
others, often for the
rest of their life.
Let us therefore raise our
children during these years
to treat everyone with love,
respect, and empathy,
understanding every life,
regardless of our differences,
is equally deserving.

Echoes in Life

There is so much noise
    and chaos in the world, it
    inhibits the quiet messages
    of our spirit within.
    Though we may sense its
    presence, it appears as an echo,
    its voice muffled in the distance,
    preventing us from clearly
    learning from its innate wisdom.
    For those who begin to question

all they were taught about life,
the chaos and loudness of
the world begins to lessen.
Everything we learned and
believed to be true is the
cause of our turmoil
and commotion.
When we genuinely
understand little we were
taught was true, the world
will become silent, as the
echoes in our life
finally disappear.

Every Life is Valuable

Every life, regardless of our
    differences or accomplishments,
    is equally important, each
    worthy of empathy, respect,
    and unconditional love.
    Though our experiences and
    personalities are different,
    inherent within each of us
    is a spirit, a piece of god,
    intimately connecting
    us to each other.
    Only by embracing this
    common bond, may we
    truly begin to understand
    our reason for being.

A Human Issue

Our thoughts, beliefs, and
    experiences, help form
    the person we become.
    Combined, they influence
    our path through life as
    we embrace prejudice,
    inequity, indifference to
    the struggles of others,
    as a normal part of life.
    The one commonality
    found in each, is that
    they are created after
    we are born, as we learn
    what is expected of us to
    survive and succeed in an
    often cruel, competitive
    self-centered world.
    Though it is important
    we understand these
    things, it is our blind
    obedience to them
    that is the cause of
    many of humanity's
    self-inflicted challenges.
    Only when we genuinely
    realize these self-centered
    beliefs hide our true purpose
    in life, to selflessly share
    our inherent wisdom and
    unconditional love, our
    spirit, with all others,

will life's many challenges
lessen, allowing the true
reason for our life's
journey to be revealed.

We Are All Brothers and Sisters

We are brought up to
believe those we have not
met, strangers, are not
important, because we are
not related or know them.
Humanity therefore ignores
these individuals, each instead
worrying only about themselves
and those closest to them.
This self-centered belief is
the reason for many of
humanity's challenges and
inequities, as the world
accepts this as its reality.
In actuality, there are no strangers.
Everyone is related by a common
purpose and connection.
We are all brothers and sisters,
intimately linked by a spirit,
a piece of god present
within each of us.
Only together, selflessly
sharing our spirit's wisdom
and unconditional love to help
each other, may we all flourish.
Apart, our life will have been
lived without meaning, as

we will have totally accepted
the isolating self-centered
illusions we first learned
when we were young.

In Darkness, See the Light

Within every life, there
is both darkness and light.
Darkness represents our
acquired values, accepted
without hesitation, as we
are taught about the self-
centered world into
which we are born.
These beliefs are the
cause of many of humanity's
struggles, negative attitudes,
and harmful ideologies
they believe are normal;
they are not.
Within each of us
though, is also light.
Light symbolizes our
original purpose, forgotten,
suppressed by our
learned egoistic beliefs.
Spirit is inherent within
every life, giving each
life purpose and meaning.
It is a choice which we
believe and will follow:
darkness or light.
We may alter our

path at any time.
Though darkness will
always remain with us,
choose to allow light
to be your primary
guide in life.
With this choice, not
only will your spirit shine
brighter, but the genuine
reason for your life's
journey will be
realized as well.

What Really Matters?

What is important?
    Is it success, wealth, family,
    material possessions, or is
    there more to life than
    our own desires?
    Though these and other
    things make our lives easier,
    they will not aid us in
    discovering our life's true purpose.
    Safety, sustenance, shelter,
    are necessary for survival.
    Most other things though,
    we desire so our life will be
    easier and more enjoyable.
    To discover life's meaning,
    find genuine happiness,
    inner peace, and true love,
    after we have secured our
    basic needs, we must then
    selflessly share our excess
    with those less fortunate,
    helping each secure their
    basic needs as well.

How Can I Help?

There are so many
    hardships experienced by
    countless people throughout

the world, it is overwhelming
to know where to begin to
try to aid others in need.
We therefore may believe
there is little we can do to
improve the lives of those
who are struggling.
This belief, encouraged by
our acceptance of the self-
centered status quo, is untrue.
Every person may change the world.
To do so, we must open our
heart, embrace the wisdom
and unconditional loving
messages we hear, then share
them, without hesitation
or cause, with all others.

The Evolution of Humanity

With the advent of
    the human race, their
    intelligence permitted
    them to become the
    dominant species on our planet.
    Though their intellect allowed
    them to discover and invent
    many things to help make
    our lives easier, and our
    knowledge of our planet
    and the universe more
    understandable, humanity's
    spiritual evolution remains
    in its infancy.
    Though there have been
    noble attempts by different
    religions to understand
    the importance of spirituality,
    organized religions eventually
    adopted man's self-centered
    interpretation of god, diluting
    the original messages and
    meaning of love, compassion,
    and concern for all, they
    were meant to convey.
    Humanity is at a crossroads.
    If they continue on their
    current path, ignoring the
    many hardships of others
    and our planet, their
    evolutionary cycle, as

so many others, may be
complete; humanity will
become a distant memory,
remembered by the skeletal
remains of their intelligence.
To prevent this potential
outcome, humanity must
selflessly help each other by
embracing our genuine spiritual
nature, present within every life,
always considering first what
is for everyone, all life, and
our planet itself, before only
worrying about what
is best for themselves.

A New Beginning

Life's challenges affect everyone.
  While wealth and privilege
  may make them easier, no
  one may escape their
  influence on our lives.
  Though those struggling
  for daily survival have
  more trials, others often
  confront fears haunting
  them from years gone by.
  It is possible to lessen
  these burdens, almost
  instantaneously, by viewing
  life through a different prism.
  For those who gaze at life
  through spiritual eyes,
  allowing their spirit, present
  within every life to be their
  primary guide, most challenges,
  regardless of cause, lessen,
  as the genuine realization of
  life's meaning, to selflessly
  share our wisdom, love,
  compassion, and excess, with
  all others, becomes clear.
  With this understanding, our
  life's journey starts anew,
  as we begin on a newfound
  path to share our spirit's
  wisdom and unconditional
  love with all others.

We Are Alive to Help Each Other

It is never acceptable
 to intentionally harm
 another in any way.
 It matters not the provocation,
 or if the injury is verbal,
 physical, emotional, or
 in any other manner.
 We are alive to support
 each other through life's
 many challenges.
 Only together will we succeed.
 Apart, though we may have
 achieved much, we will have
 overlooked the genuine
 purpose for our life's journey.

A Moment of Grace

Perhaps if we stop for
 a moment, quiet our
 minds, listen to the quiet
 soothing loving messages
 within, we may experience
 a meaningful reflection,
 an echo of a time before
 we were exposed
 to life's illusions.
 What we would witness
 is a world where our
 directive is to genuinely

care, help, and love each
other, regardless of our
differences, by selflessly
sharing our spirit's
wisdom and unconditional
love to help all others.
This moment of grace is
reflective of our life's
true mission; it is the
reason we are born,
the meaning of life.

The Beauty of Life

When you look at another,
    what do you see?
    Do you see their appearance,
    flaws, or do you see the pure
    beauty of their soul within?
    Every person, regardless of
    our differences, is perfect.
    Discard their outer layer,
    the façade we see, to
    view the genuine beauty
    that has always been
    present within each.

Every Life is Equally Valuable

We are alive to selflessly
    share our innate wisdom
    and unconditional love,
    our spirit, with all others.
    It matters not beliefs,
    appearance, wealth, genus,
    or any other comparisons
    we may make.
    Every life, regardless of our
    differences, is connected,
    intimately linked together
    by the spirit, a piece of
    god present within each.
    Each life, therefore,
    is equally valuable.
    Only when humanity truly
    embraces this belief, realizing
    the self-centered matrix we are
    living in is an illusion, may
    the spiritual evolution of
    our planet finally begin.

Our Symbiotic Relationship

Sense the beauty, aroma
    of nature, of every life
    intimately connected to
    each other, existing on
    our extraordinary planet.

See the radiance, their aura,
vibrate from their core, as
each life networks, coming
alive in their interactions.
Every part of our planet,
every life on it, has a
symbiotic relationship
with each other.
The loss of one, no
matter how insignificant,
effects all.
Only together, acknowledging
the importance and equal
right of each to exist,
may our world spiritually
evolve, mitigating many
of the innumerable
challenges humanity
has created for itself.

Friendship

Friendship is opening
    your heart to another, a
    stranger even, without intent.
    Every life has a universal
    purpose: to discover our
    mutual spirit, present
    within each, then share
    it to benefit all.
    Spirit represents pure love,
    untouched by humanity's
    self-centered definition,
    meant unite us as one.
    With this understanding,
    we will realize there
    are no strangers.
    We are all friends, alive
    to selflessly share our
    spirit's inherent wisdom
    and unconditional love,
    reminding each to accept
    all others as friends as well.

Our Light

Untethered by man's
    interference, the intensity
    of the light, present
    within each, is blinding.
    Its luminous rays penetrate
    everything it touches, leaving
    pure love in its wake.
    With our birth though, our
    light begins to dim as we
    learn and accept the beliefs
    of the self-centered world
    in which we are to live.
    We then may spend the
    rest of our life, trying to
    rediscover the vibrant
    intensity of our light,
    our infinite ability to
    share our love, our light,
    with the world once more.

A Moment in Time

Our life may change instantly.
    If we open our heart, listen
    to the silence in between our
    racing thoughts, and embrace
    the soft tender messages
    emanating from our core,
    we may awaken to the
    genuine possibilities
    life truly offers.
    By selflessly sharing
    the innate wisdom and
    unconditional loving
    messages we sense, at
    that very moment, our
    self-centered views,
    beliefs, and prejudices
    will begin to dissipate,
    as we begin on an
    enduring journey to
    discover our life's
    true purpose.

Everyone Has Value

We each will have many
    challenges during our lives
    that influence the path,
    actions, and direction,
    our life will take.

For some, the struggles
they face may be
overwhelming, as they
battle the harsh
realities life present.
Despite our differences
or circumstances in life
though, every person
has value and must
not be abandoned.
Though it may be
difficult to be near
someone we consider
unworthy of our time or
friendship, we each
may help change the
direction of another
by selflessly sharing
our love, our spirit
with them, intimately
linking us together.
This one simple act
can change the direction
of their life forever, as
it may trigger them to
awaken, beginning
them on a journey
to remember their
original purpose in life.

We Each May Change the World

We must not wait,
    rely on another to
    act, magically hoping
    life will improve for
    those who are struggling,
    suffering from living
    in an indifferent self-
    centered world.
    Every person, no matter
    our differences or lack of
    resources, may change
    the direction of the world.
    To do so, open your heart,
    then selflessly share the
    wisdom and infinite love
    waiting your permission
    to be released.

We Each Must Rely on Another

Every life, regardless
    of our differences,
    accomplishments, or
    genus, is an important
    meaningful part of the world.
    Since humanity is the dominant
    lifeform, they believe they have
    the right to cause grievous
    harm to other forms of life,

each other, and the planet
that sustains us all.
This self-centered belief is the
underlying cause for many of
humanity's needless problems,
hardships, and challenges.
In truth, every life, is equally
vital, part of an ecosystem
in which we each must
rely on the other.
Senseless injury to
one life, injures all.
Until humanity genuinely
realizes this, the continuing
damage they have and will
continue to do to our planet
and all who live on it,
may prove irreparable.

Before We Can Fix the World

There are many
   challenges in the world.
   Though some problems
   we cannot fix, there
   are many others
   created by humanity.
   War, hunger, prejudice,
   inequity, are just a few of
   the man-made difficulties
   and harmful emotions
   affecting countless every day.
   There are some who have

tried, frequently in vain,
to alleviate the
struggles of others.
Unfortunately, these
solutions are often temporary,
not fixing the underlying
cause, the self-centered
world in which we live.
Before we may fix the
world and truly help others,
we must first change
ourselves, by embracing
and accepting the inherent
wisdom and messages
of unconditional love
within, then selflessly
sharing those messages,
without motive or
benefit, with all others.
Only then, may our world
finally evolve, assuring a
future for every life
and our planet itself.

The End

Though our mortal body
has a beginning and finite
end, our spirit, a piece
of god accompanying
every life, is immortal.
With death, our physical
body withers as its remains

are cremated or buried.
Our essence, however, who
we truly were when alive,
moves to a higher vibrational
plane, where it joins others,
until called upon once more,
to join another sentient life.
A small part of our
essence, however, also
continues to exist in the
hearts and soul of all
those it influenced
during its last incarnation.
Every interaction we
have, when joined with
a sentient life, regardless
how brief, may influence
the direction of countless others.
Though our body will
perish, our essence will
continue to live forever
in all those we met and
inspired during our brief
sojourn through life.

~ ~

About the Author

My name is Ken Luball. Spiritual Seeker ~ Author ~ Guide.
** Author of "The Awakening Tetralogy: A series of Four Spiritual Books".
****

Ever since I was a young child, I knew my purpose in life; it was to Awaken, find Enlightenment, and share my experience and knowledge with others. To reach those lofty aspirations though, I first had to navigate through quite a few unexpected detours in my life. It was not until after I stopped following a formal religion, I finally was able to embrace *Spirituality*, and with this embrace, I *Awoke*.

Spirituality is the belief there is a piece of God (a *Spirit*) within everything that has life, and, because of this, all life is important, equal, and connected.

It took me almost an entire lifetime to become to be *Awakened* and begin my journey towards *Enlightenment*.

After I Awoke I realized everything I had *Learned* throughout my life was untrue. I had looked for love and happiness in the job I had, the money I made, things I owned, and through my wife and children. With the exception of the latter, I finally realized none of those things truly mattered.

I knew Enlightenment was a gift to be shared with others. That is my destiny. Therefore, I have written "The Awakening Tetralogy", a series of four "Spiritual" books. It is my hope by reading these books, you will begin a new adventure. One where you will *Awaken* and further your journey towards *Enlightenment* with your Spirit Within.

Read more at kenluball.com.

www.ingramcontent.com/pod-product-compliance
Lightning Source LLC
Chambersburg PA
CBHW030329180626
46810CB00003B/1280